MEDICINE BIRD

By Sharon Greene

and Jacen Greene

ISBN 978-0-9857616-1-5

MEDICINE BIRD

Chapter One: Summer, 1995

Harriet Frazier tipped a generous portion of whisky from a flask into her steaming cup of tea.

"Whiskey, Nat?" she asked.

Natalie Hughes shook her head and held her hand protectively over her own cup of tea.

"Not even to celebrate your bachelorette status?" asked Harriet, the corner of her mouth twitching in a half-smile almost hidden amongst her wrinkles.

"Now isn't the time to start. Besides, it's been almost a year."

"You hardly act like it," said Harriet. She put the whiskey flask away high in the cupboard. "I know what I'd be doing if I still had dark hair, high cheekbones, and a perky butt like yours."

"Harriet!"

Harriet chuckled.

"It's just too early, is all," said Natalie, blowing steam off her tea and rolling the cup in her hands.

"Lemon and honey?"

"Just lemon, thanks."

"I only keep the honey for you, so you'd better use it," Harriet said in mock frustration.

"Not today. I'm in a sour mood."

"Very well."

Harriet took a lemon from a basket hanging over the sink, sliced it in two on the cutting board, and gave half to Natalie.

"Aren't you going to sit down?" asked Natalie as she squeezed the lemon into her tea.

"You know I don't like clutter in the kitchen," said Harriet, placing the other half of the lemon into the old, metal-handed refrigerator and wiping off the cutting board. Natalie watched her old friend and new landlord for a moment, trying to hide a grin as Harriet stood with her hands on her hips, surveying the kitchen like a drill sergeant inspecting a barracks. Satisfied that nothing more could be done to clean the spotless surfaces, Harriet plopped into a chair, her flyaway gray hair bouncing with the movement.

"You should have some fun," said Harriet, trying and failing to sound offhand.

"I am having fun. I like rooming with you."

"Well, you're the only person I know who enjoys drinking tea with saggy old women."

"I'm going out to do today's count. That's always relaxing."

"My no-good grandson is also around today, so watch out for straying eyes."

"I hardly think he'd be interested in a… a divorced older woman."

Harriet shrugged innocently. "I don't think those are the first things on his mind."

Natalie gulped the rest of her tea, holding the cup high to hide her flushed cheeks. "I have to go."

"I know how those egrets hate to be kept waiting."

Natalie stood and washed her cup at the sink, then hung it carefully in the rack to dry. "I'll be back later."

"Oh, don't bother," Harriet said with a wave of one liver-spotted hand. "Duffy will be by, and I don't want any competition."

Natalie grinned. Duffy was a few years older than Harriet, nearly twice Natalie's age.

"Okay, then," said Natalie. "Maybe he'll use some of that honey."

"He hates tea!"

"What about whiskey?"

"That might work."

"Have fun."

Natalie grabbed her bag and walked out the kitchen door. She stood for a moment on the back porch of the tall Victorian, the "Blue Heron Bed and Breakfast," and shivered in the damp morning air. A craftsman bungalow stood on the other side of the gravel driveway, in the shade of a stand of tall firs. Through a gap in the rhododendrons at the end of the driveway, Natalie could see Qualawalu Bay, fog rising in long tendrils from the winding sloughs and inlets.

She strolled quickly down the path toward the bay, between tall, dripping grasses where spider webs lay heavy with water. Past the last bleached shell of the neglected outbuildings, the hills sloped steeply down to the reedy shore where Natalie's kayak lay overturned. When she reached the kayak, something—a noise, an odd feeling—made her look back at the blue roof and tall, double-hung windows of the old Victorian farmhouse far up the slope.

A dark, sudden wave of depression fell across Natalie, crashing through her mind. She fought a rising sense of panic, the sensation so familiar now after the divorce, struggling to regain control. She closed her eyes, stood on one leg like an egret, and held her palms slightly apart. As she turned in a slow, ballet-like motion, she breathed deeply in and felt the darkness, the fear, receding away from her like a falling tide. The familiar patterns of Tai Chi relaxed her muscles and quieted her thoughts. In a moment, she opened her eyes again and turned away from the old house.

A few hours later, the dark thoughts of the morning were nothing more than a disquieting murmur in the back of Natalie's mind as she pulled her kayak out of the water and flipped it over, finished with that day's bird count. Nearly finished, anyway. Out in the slough, a slender egret stood frozen in the shallow water, head bent at an angle, neck extended forward as it waited for tiny fish to appear. A background of dark green rushes formed a sharp contrast to the white bird. Natalie hurriedly screwed a 200-millimeter lens onto her camera and steadied it on her upside-down kayak.

As the egret resolved into focus through the viewfinder, Natalie heard the sharp bark of a dog directly behind her. The egret lifted from the water in a blur of flapping wings and disappeared out of the frame. Looking up, she watched it fly over the reeds toward the wide bay beyond, dark legs trailing below like a memory of its flight.

A large black Labrador bounded out of the reeds and onto the muddy shore. He ran to Natalie, tail wagging and tongue lolling as if expecting a reward for chasing off the egret. She pushed him away and stood up.

"Get off, Waldo. You're filthy."

The Lab lay down in the grass, his eyes begging forgiveness. A figure emerged from the tall brush behind him.

"Sorry about that. Didn't know you were here, Nat."

Ron Frazier stood above her, backlit by the late afternoon sun. Natalie unscrewed the heavy lens and put it in her pack.

"That's all right. I'll try again tomorrow." She tried to smile politely, hoping it would mask the irritation in her voice. She hated when he called her Nat, but her anger vanished with his disarming grin. Then she was angry with herself for not being irritated at him.

"How's the bird count?" asked Ron. "Fish and Wildlife getting their money's worth?"

"Money well spent, thanks, but I'm done for the day."

"Can we walk you back?"

"If you carry my gear."

He held out his hands, and she gave him her spotting scope and the double-bladed kayak paddle. She pulled the kayak further up on the bank, wiped the mud off of her shoes, and pulled on her pack.

The path followed the slough, cutting through tall grass until it reached a place where a barbed wire fence blocked the way, marking the boundary of the Frazier farm. Ron went over first and held the wire down for Natalie. From there Waldo led the way, racing through the lupine and coyote brush of a steep slope that ended at a large pasture.

As she climbed, Natalie absentmindedly studied the muscles of Ron's back under his faded orange T-shirt. She liked his dark hair and angular features, so different from her ex-husband. At least in appearance.

"The dig is going well," said Ron, glancing back at Natalie. She quickly averted her eyes, hoping he hadn't noticed her staring.

"Find anything good?" asked Natalie.

"Bits and pieces. Harriet will want to look at all of 'em before I can take anything, though. You know how she is about her collection."

"It's her land."

"And I'm the one digging all day and eating tinned beans every night. You can imagine how bad it is sleeping in a tent after that." Ron grinned and leaned the kayak paddle against a tall cypress tree at the top of the hill. He threw a stick for Waldo and the Lab dashed off across the pasture. Natalie sat down in the shade of the tree.

Qualawalu Bay stretched north for miles below. The incoming tide flowed into a network of sloughs and estuaries that branched through the surrounding wetlands like the arteries of some huge animal. Where a vast expanse of intertidal salt marsh had been drained for pasture, a herd of Black Angus grazed. White egrets stood sentinel among the cattle, waiting to impale mice or voles stirred up by wandering hooves.

"Beautiful, isn't it?" asked Ron.

"It has a special feeling," said Natalie, plucking a foxtail and twirling it in her hand. She glanced up to see him watching her and felt oddly self-conscious. "Daoists believe the universe is held in balance by opposing forces, yin and yang. I think that's why the bay is so peaceful. It's a perfect balance between the pounding ocean and the yielding land. I like to come here to meditate."

"And to practice Tai Chi?"

"You've been spying on me."

"Sorry. It was unintentional—I was just out for a morning walk."

They were both silent for a moment.

"It was a beautiful sequence," said Ron. "I learned a short form years ago, but it was nothing like yours."

"My teacher is a awful old Chinese woman, and I love her dearly. She's determined to set me straight, whatever that means. Says I live too much in my head."

He laughed. "Don't we all."

Waldo brought the stick back. Ron picked it up and pointed to the land below. "My dad has plans for that lower pasture. Says the Coastal Commission will let him re-zone and turn this farm into a fancy housing development. It's depressing."

Natalie's stomach tightened. "That area is a seasonal wetland for migrating waterfowl." She felt herself gearing up for a lecture, stopped. No need. Ron was an ally. "The birds are overcrowded as it is. I don't think Fish and Wildlife would allow development, especially once my numbers are in."

"Maybe. I heard Fish and Wildlife has been trying to purchase it for years as a buffer for the refuge," he said. "If someone sold them part of the land, they might be less prone to interfere."

"And the Coastal Commission? Does he have that all wrapped up as well?"

Ron shrugged. "He has a friend on the Coastal Commission, knows how to pull strings in the governor's office. The only person standing in his way is Harriet. He's been trying to talk her into approving the project, letting him manage it now instead of waiting until he inherits." He turned to look at her. "Has she spoken to you about wanting to deed the farm to the Nature Conservancy?"

"We've talked about it, but I didn't give her the idea," said Natalie. "It was the avian cholera epidemic last spring that made her think of it. She went out every day to the ponds in the pasture and helped pull out dead ducks 'til it was over."

"She's going to see her attorney tomorrow," said Ron.

Natalie turned away to hide her smile of relief. "Twelve hundred acres is a lot of land. People won't be happy."

"No kidding. She's planning to put in a no grazing clause. To top that off, she's selling sixty acres to the Indians for half its value. If she goes through with it, there'll be a family battle that'll make last Christmas look like a tea party."

"What happened at Christmas?"

"Dad and Aunt Helen went for each other's jugulars over something I can't even remember. Mom got drunk, as usual, and Harriet ran weeping to her bedroom. I took her a hot toddy, and we sat and reminisced until it got dark. One of the best times I ever spent with her."

"Does everyone in the family call her Harriet?"

"Everyone. I stopped calling her grandma when I was fourteen."

Natalie rose and brushed off her slacks. "I'm starving. I think I remember some blueberry muffins left over from breakfast. Want to join me for tea?"

He nodded and stood up. Waldo jumped up and led the way across the pasture, into the trail between rhododendrons that let onto the circular drive.

"She's probably in the house making tea," Ron said as they crossed the gravel driveway.

He bounded up the steps of the back porch and called through the screen door. No one answered. He looked at Natalie questioningly. "Theresa's pickup isn't here. Shouldn't she be getting dinner ready? I wonder if there are any guests arriving."

Natalie was gripped with a sudden sense of anxiety. As Ron wiped Waldo's paws on the doormat, Natalie opened the door and stepped into the kitchen. Sunlight streamed through the windows into the living room beyond, directly on Harriet Frazier. She sat dozing in a wingback chair, her mouth hanging open, silver hair backlit by the window.

There was a dark spot on Harriet's head, too wet to be merely shadow.

Natalie rushed to the old woman's side, bending down to put an ear against her slumped chest. No heartbeat. Harriet Frazier was dead.

Chapter Two: Murder

The screen door slammed behind Natalie.

"Oh my God! Harriet!"

Ron rushed to Natalie's side, knelt down, felt for a pulse. "Quick, call an ambulance!"

"She's gone, Ron. I think she's been dead for awhile." There was a strange clarity in Natalie's thoughts, a distance from her own self and her emotions.

"But how?"

"I'm not sure, but the wound on her head didn't come from a fall. I think someone killed her."

"This is insane. I can't believe it."

Natalie moved to the phone and dialed 911. She felt as though she might vomit as she gave the dispatcher directions to the house. Ron held Harriet's lifeless palm to his cheek, closed his eyes and silently wept.

Natalie put the receiver down. "I'm going to wait outside. I can't stay in here. I feel faint."

Ron stood and headed for the hallway. "I should check the other rooms—see if anything was taken."

"Don't touch anything. Okay?"

"I won't."

Natalie's arms and legs felt like lead, hanging heavily, pulling her down. She leaned against the doorway to the kitchen, holding her mouth. When the nausea receded, she walked into the kitchen for a glass of water. Her gaze fell on a Ball canning jar on the windowsill. Inside were strips of bark. She'd never noticed it before. From the skin it appeared to be willow, light with dark striations, and it was fresh.

She looked around. In the drainer a trio of porcelain cups lay tilted to dry. The honey jar was out. Harriet's friend Duffy must have stopped by earlier that afternoon.

Outside, Ron sat on the porch steps with his hands over his face. Natalie sat down beside him, put a hand on his shoulder.

"I want to think this is a nightmare. That I'll wake up any minute," he said.

Natalie wanted to scream, to jump up and run until she collapsed, until the image of Harriet's lifeless body was pushed from her mind. She sat in silence and waited.

A siren wailed in the distance. Fern Valley, the nearest small town, was a fifteen-minute drive away. Ten minutes at high speed. The sheriff's car careened into the driveway, lights flashing. A deputy climbed out. Ron stood up and showed him into the house. A few minutes later, an ambulance appeared. Two EMTs jumped out. Natalie motioned them inside.

She sat on the porch, listening to the chatter in the house, the squawk of the sheriff's radio from the patrol car. There was the sound of another engine, the crunch of tires on gravel. Natalie glanced up, wondering who would be the next to arrive too late.

A dirty black pickup with fluorescent pink windshield wipers pulled up behind the ambulance, blocking it in. Theresa Bergstrom, a teenage neighbor and sometime employee of Harriet's, climbed out of the pickup. The daughter of a local rancher, Theresa had an angular, serious face, blonde hair tied back in a ponytail, and the lean muscles of someone accustomed to working with cattle.

"Has something happened?" she asked. "Where's Harriet?"

Natalie rose and put a hand on Theresa's shoulder. "Don't go inside, okay? Promise me you won't look."

"What happened?" An edge of panic crept into Theresa's voice.

"She's dead. Someone killed her."

Theresa's reaction was far calmer than Harriet had expected. The girl turned away and stared out at the fields that lay between the house and the bay. "It's not right," she said, shaking her head. "This can't be true."

"Weren't you supposed to be working here this afternoon?"

"Harriet said I could have the rest of the day off—Mr. Duffy was coming. You know, that friend of hers from Forest Glen." Theresa paused and lowered her voice. "Do you think he did it?"

"I have no idea, but I'm sure the sheriff will want to know if Harriet had a visitor. For now, why don't you go home and tell your parents? They should know about this. Who knows what this murdered wanted, or if they're still around." Natalie guided Theresa back into her pickup. "Can you drive?"

"Yes. It's only a mile. I'm okay. It's just... it's not..." Theresa hung her head, her fingers wrapped tightly around the wheel.

The girl was in shock—or nervous. Natalie couldn't tell which. She watched as Theresa drove quickly away.

The sheriff's deputy walked out onto the porch.

"Who was that?" he asked.

"Just the neighbor's daughter. She cleaned for Harriet."

"She should have stayed," he said with a tone of gentle admonishment. "I'll need to get her name and address from you."

"Of course." Natalie nodded.

"We're waiting for a detective, Sergeant Davis. He's on his way from Clam Beach. Should be here in about twenty minutes. Can't move the body 'til then."

"Can I go inside and pack my things?"

"Not 'til Sergeant Davis gets here."

Natalie sat down on the edge of the porch, twisting her hands together, and stared at the gravel drive. Tiny blades of grass pushed up through the pebbles. Pieces of a broken seashell lay strewn to one side of the porch steps. There was clarity to Natalie's focus, a narrowing of vision that threw everything into heightened relief. And yet there was darkness at the edge of her vision, and a mirroring darkness in her thoughts, a wall that held back a tumult of thoughts and emotions.

Natalie turned her hands over and stared at the new-seeming wrinkles on their back, the web of branching veins like the estuaries of the bay. She began to cry, her face in her hands, and realized that she was crying not for Harriet, but for herself.

A green Ford sedan with a whip antenna attached to the hood pulled into the driveway. A man with thick gray hair, wearing a suit and tie, stepped out. He pulled a large bag from the back seat as the deputy stepped forward with a greeting. They chatted for a moment, glancing occasionally at Natalie, then walked to the porch.

"Ma'am," the man said with a nod, then followed the deputy into the house.

Natalie waited on the porch with her hands in her lap, feeling foolish for not stepping inside and introducing herself, but sick at the thought of seeing Harriet's corpse again. Who could do such a thing? Her mind raced through the possibilities. The Bergstroms, Theresa's parents, leased land for grazing that they would lose if Harriet split the property between the local Wiyot tribe and the Nature Conservancy. Richard, Harriet's son, wouldn't have been able to pursue his planned development if she had lived. Helen, Harriet's daughter, a wealthy accountant who lived in the Bay Area, apparently detested her mother. Maybe Harriet had cancer and her boyfriend, Duffy, had killed her out of a misguided sense of charity. Maybe Ron had killed Harriet so he could dig up the rest of her property looking for artifacts. Maybe a wandering maniac had done it.

It was impossible even to guess what had happened, and why, but Natalie had to know. It would do so much just to quiet her own fear if the murder could be explained, categorized, described like the behaviors of the birds she watched. Animals never did anything without purpose. Surely humans didn't either.

The door to the house slammed shut behind Natalie. She stood and turned as the gray-haired man reached out and shook her hand firmly. He had a kind face, an intense look in his dark eyes.

"You must be Miss Hughes. Ron Frazier said you were with him when he found the body. I'm Baxter Davis; most people call me Buck. I'll be investigating this case. We'll be taking a statement from you later. How well did you know Mrs. Frazier?""

"Pretty well. I met her two years ago, when I was tracking some pelicans with radio collars. This summer she offered me a room at a low rate because I'm working at the Wildlife Refuge on a temporary assignment. She was like… an aunt, or a second mother. I don't know. A friend."

Davis pulled a pack of cigarettes from his pocket, held it out to Natalie. She shook her head, no. He tapped one out of the pack, lit it, inhaled deeply.

"Do you have any idea of who might have wanted to kill her? There's no sign of a struggle or burglary. The car is still in the garage. It looks like someone simply walked up behind her and killed her with a single blow."

"I… I noticed someone had tea. There's a cup in the drainer, still wet, and honey out on the counter. Harriet didn't use honey. She was expecting a friend this afternoon, but he hardly sounds like a murder suspect. Kind of a doddering old birder, a couple years older than Harriet, seventy-six, I think. I doubt if he has the strength to kill anyone." She gave the detective Duffy's name, and he added it to a list on a small pad of paper.

"He might have seen someone. We'll check it out," said Davis.

Natalie crossed her arms across her chest and bit at her lower lip. "What about the murder weapon?"

"Looks like a heavy instrument, something with an edge, not as sharp as a hoe, but similar."

The EMTs guided a gurney out the door and carried it down the steps. The covered body was strapped tightly to the top. They slid the gurney through the open doors of the ambulance, then drove slowly away. Pink rose bushes reached with arching branches into the road, brushing against the sides of the vehicle, almost as if they were saying good-bye.

"Are you going to be all right, Ma'am?" Davis looked concerned.

"I think the shock is wearing off. Maybe I should be alone."

"Ron Frazier is calling the family. I'll be around for a couple hours. We may need to ask you a few more questions. Are you planning to leave right away?"

"Probably not until tomorrow."

"Be sure to lock up tight. Most of these cases involve someone who was close to the victim and had a simple motive for wanting her out of the way. But there's always the possibility of a transient, some lunatic passing through the area. We only have one deputy patrolling the southern part of the county during each shift. Budget cuts. I can't promise you much protection out here. Do you have a gun?"

"No." She had a fleeting memory of the automatic pistol Mark, her husband, had bought, after a burglar had broken into the neighbor's house. She had held the cold piece of steel only once, overcome with a sick feeling as she thought of the weapon's sole purpose. She had told him she didn't want the gun in the house. The incident had led to another heated argument. He had won, of course.

Davis gave her his card. "Call me if you think of anything else. If we don't find the murder weapon tonight, we'll be back with some deputies in the morning to search a wider area."

She looked across the yard to where the deputy was stretching yellow crime scene ribbon around the porch of the house.

"Why would someone kill a helpless old lady?" whispered Natalie.

"I don't know." Davis rubbed his chin and looked her steadily in the eyes. "Someone who was desperate. Maybe someone who was angry about the will. Could be a family member. We'll do our best to find out, Miss Hughes. You can count on it."

Ron appeared on the porch of the house. He had a lost look on his face, his eyes wide with sorrow. Waldo, who had been sniffing the weeds next to the fence, saw him, picked up a small stick, and carried it to him. The dog nuzzled his master's hand, but Ron seemed not to notice. He walked slowly down the stairs and came to Natalie.

"I called everyone who needs to know. I'm going back to my dig to be alone. My parents and Helen will be here tomorrow."

"I'll be here tonight if you need me, Ron." She put a hand on his shoulder.

He looked back at the house. His eyes grew cold and angry. "If I find who did this, they'll never make it to trial."

It was a strangely ineffective threat, thought Natalie, like a line from a bad movie. "Could you bring yourself to kill someone?"

He bent down and took the stick from Waldo's jaw, inspected it for a moment, then hurled it far out over the driveway. Wiping his hands, he turned and fixed Natalie with a chilling gaze.

"Yes," he said, "yes, I could."

Chapter Three: The Message

It was late in the evening before Natalie was let back into the house. As she climbed the staircase to her room, she paused and ran her hand along the polished redwood banister. Most of the furnishings in the Blue Heron Bed and Breakfast were antiques, some threadbare, an effect unglamorous but oddly comforting.

In her room on the second floor, Natalie sat down in a wingback chair beside a tall window. Her ability to vividly recall scenes and conversations from the past had often been a curse, especially after the divorce. She had once read that memory was always linked to feeling, and often her attempts to control the images penetrating her mind proved futile, and sometimes painful. Now, as images of her friendship with Harriet sprang into her consciousness, she found them comforting. In this way she could almost recreate Harriet, alive and smiling, in defiance of her murderer.

In the first weeks after Mark had left Natalie, when she had missed him the most, longing for one more touch, she found she could evoke his image quite clearly. But it had slowly faded until one day when she no longer remembered his face. It would surely be the same with Harriet, but for now, Natalie desperately wanted to feel the presence of her dear friend one last time, even if it was only a fantasy.

Their friendship had begun two years earlier, when Natalie had come to Qualawalu Bay following a pair of brown pelicans as part of a research project. The birds had been rehabilitated and harnessed with radio transmitters after the American Trader oil spill at Huntington Beach, then tracked by radio telemetry for a year to see how they fared. The harnesses were designed to fall off after that time. Two years later a biologist at the Qualawalu National Wildlife Refuge spotted a pair of pelicans with harnesses still in place. Natalie drove up to net them at night, where they roosted on some old pilings, and remove the harnesses.

On her first day out Natalie took a wrong turn driving back from the bay and spotted the Blue Heron sign. It was May. Masses of bright pink rhododendrons bordered the yard, hiding the first floor of the old Victorian. A heady scent of lilacs filled the air, and tiny finches beeped at one another as they hopped between the branches of a huge, trailing rose bush.

Climbing out of her van, Natalie took a deep breath of the cool salt air. Someone called to her from an enclosed garden, and Natalie turned to see the face of an elderly woman peering over a fence covered with passionflower vines.

Tall, with short, white hair and softly wrinkled skin, Harriet Frazier wore baggy tan slacks and a long-sleeved cotton shirt. Natalie guessed Harriet to be at least seventy. The old woman held her back straight, her head high. Her eyes sparkled, and her smile was genuine and warm as she greeted Natalie at the garden gate with a firm handshake.

Harriet picked up a pile of weeds and flung them over the fence, then walked across a border of lemon thyme, releasing a delicious scent from the plants crushed with each step. She beckoned Natalie to follow her through an arching trellis of roses that led into the front yard of the Blue Heron Bed and Breakfast.

It was the smell of the place that had first drawn Natalie to the Blue Heron. The musty odor of aged redwood and oak mixed with a faint scent of furniture oil. It conveyed a feeling of permanence and security. She followed Harriet through the house, awestruck by the little flourishes and grand spaces of the structure, a house built entirely of old-growth redwood.

Harriet chatted to Natalie as she showed her the rooms. The land had been a dairy until Harriet's husband, Nathan, had died ten years before. She had leased the bottomland for grazing and turned the old Victorian into a bed and breakfast in the summer. There were four bedrooms upstairs, three of them large, but a smaller one in back, Harriet's favorite, seemed perfect for Natalie.

Natalie had stayed for a week, then returned occasionally for weekends. She and Harriet exchanged letters, and Harriet became a trusted friend. When Harriet wrote to her that the local wildlife refuge needed a temporary biologist, Natalie had leapt at the chance. It was a special place to Natalie, and it held no memory of Mark.

The noise of men's voices outside pulled Natalie from her reverie. Odd, she thought, opening her eyes, how the mind holds such a vivid image after someone dies. She could almost feel Harriet's presence, smell her sweet scent, like talcum. The reality of her loss hit Natalie again, and her stomach tightened as if it had been struck. As she raised her hands to her face, her shoulders began to heave, and she let go of the sobs welling up in her chest.

That evening, after picking at a tasteless dinner, Natalie packed her things. She stepped out of the house and walked across the pasture to Harriet's favorite spot for watching the sunset, an outcropping of chert at the top of a bluff by the ocean. One cluster of rocks created a seat far enough from the edge to allay Natalie's fear of heights.

Natalie watched the shimmering orange globe of the sun melt into the ocean, feathery clouds above turning an iridescent pink, then lavender, as the light faded. An incoming tide sent huge waves crashing against the rocks below, filling the air with a salty spray. A line of pelicans winged their way homeward in single file, their large, elegant heads curved regally back on their necks.

As she stood to leave, Natalie noticed something red wedged between the rocks: a book. A letter was stuck inside, with her name clearly written on the envelope. Her hands shook as she took it out. It was from Harriet.

"My dear Nat," it read. "I am leaving this letter here, at our rock, because I think I am in danger. My fears may be groundless, but I'm playing it safe. I have written a new will. Can't trust my attorney. Two witnesses I do trust have signed it. It is hidden in a safe place, and I'm counting on you to stay until it surfaces. It is inside the blue heron. I know this must be a mystery, but you like mysteries, and I hope it will keep you occupied for a while. This land should go back to its first owners, and I am at peace knowing I have filled my duty to the spirits that live here.

"Don't let the neighbors and relatives call me a crazy old woman. And don't let Carol Bergstrom steal my roses for the county fair! My floribundas are the best they've ever been. If I'm not here to enter them, I want you to do it for me. Love, Harriet. P.S., go out on a date sometime."

Natalie's stomach tightened with a feeling of apprehension and excitement. A new will! Harriet had outwitted her enemy, had known she had an enemy. Why hadn't she named that person? And what did she mean about the will surfacing? That was an odd choice of words. Who were the two witnesses? Unanswered questions swarmed in her mind, too fast to contemplate one at a time. First Harriet's death, and now this overwhelming task to put things right. It would take time to sort things out.

Natalie put the letter and the little book in the pocket of her jacket. It was growing quickly darker, and the Victorian was mostly dark without someone there to turn on the lights. She stopped. A light flickered in the ground floor. At first, Natalie thought it was a reflection from the headlights of a passing car, but she realized the angle was wrong. It shone again in the window of the study. A flashlight.

Natalie broke into a run along the path. As she neared the house, a figure disappeared into the darkness of the pasture, walking quickly toward the road. In the gathering dusk it was too dim to tell who it was, even whether it was a man or a woman. She stood still, listening for the sound of a car starting. When she heard nothing, she decided to go inside. Whoever it was had come on foot.

The back door to the house stood open. Natalie switched on the lights and looked around. The kitchen and living room seemed to be in order, but in the study, Harriet's desk drawers were open. Books lay strewn on the floor, and a manila folder was open on the desk, the pages it had held scattered. She gathered them up, careful to touch only the bottom edge of each page. She read a few lines, piecing them together by page number. They were Harriet's handwritten memoirs. Was this what the intruder had wanted?

She left the folder untouched on the desk and took the pages with her. Her curiosity and the possibility of finding a clue to the hiding place of the will made it impossible to wait to read them.

Back in the kitchen, Natalie sat down at the table and skimmed the pages. Harriet had written rambling recollections over a period of months in a stiff, formal style. There were two distinct breaks in the writing where pages seemed to be missing.

A rustling sound outside the window brought a prickly feeling to her spine. She tensed, imagining someone watching her. The cat door snapped shut, and Harriet's yellow tabby mrow-wowed for its dinner. Natalie heaved a sigh of relief and checked to make certain the back door was bolted shut.

Someone knocked on the front door, and she jumped.

"Natalie! It's me, Ron."

She unfastened the dead bolt and let Ron in. Waldo bounded past his legs. She led the way into the kitchen, unable to keep from talking.

"Ron, someone was in the house! I saw a flashlight, and Harriet left a letter for me, and there's a new will. We have to call Davis."

Ron examined the pages on the table without sitting down. She pulled the letter from her pocket and handed it to him. His eyes widened as he read.

"I can't believe she pulled this off. We'll have to find it, of course."

"Why do you think she said the will would surface? That seems like such an odd choice of words."

"She was an odd woman," said Ron. He handed the letter back to Natalie and sorted idly through the pages on the table. "I do know the attorney, Wayne Baumeister. Carol Bergstrom is his sister. Conflict of interest there, just a little?"

"The part about the roses seemed unusual. I didn't know Harriet was so competitive."

Ron looked up and smiled. "Nothing was trivial when it came to her arch rival. Carol tried to steal some cuttings from Harriet's roses years ago. I guess she thought Harriet had developed some super strain that was fog-hardy, resisted black spot, made coffee for you in the morning, whatever. Harriet's roses won at the fair every year. She has a drawer full of blue ribbons."

"Doesn't it seem odd she was concerned about winning ribbons when her life was being threatened?"

"Maybe it's a clue to the location of the will. I don't suppose there's a type of rose called a blue heron?"

"I don't think so, but Harriet always kept the foil tags on them. It's worth checking."

"We should do a search. Room by room. Want to start tonight?" He glanced around the room.

"I'd rather have a glass of wine and search in the morning when my head is clear." She found a half empty bottle of Chablis in the refrigerator and poured two glasses. Ron sat down at the table across from her.

"Did her letter convince you to stay on for a few days?"

"I don't know. I feel spooked. I tense at the slightest noise. I keep expecting Harriet to walk into the room any minute. I hate the thought of being here alone." She stopped, felt her cheeks redden.

"I could move my stuff up here. Would that make you feel safer?"

His concern made her want to reach out and touch his hand. She shifted her gaze away and took a breath. Better to take things slowly. "How about leaving Waldo? He could sleep inside the front door."

"Sure. He's a good watchdog, but don't let him in your room unless you don't mind the smell of dog farts." Ron scratched Waldo's head.

"Right. I'll watch out for that," said Natalie. "By the way, how well do you know the Bergstroms?"

"Their ancestors homesteaded here at the same time as ours, sometime back in the Stone Age. Jack Bergstrom has a bad temper, used to drink, but I heard he stopped a few years ago. I can't picture him as a killer—he has a kind of redneck integrity." He took a sip of wine. "Harriet was very fond of you. She told me you'd had a hard time since your divorce."

"He left me for someone else. Things weren't good between us, but it was still devastating. You know, the marriage brought our parts of myself I didn't even know existed. Harriet suggested I take the job at the bay to put things behind me."

"I broke up with my fiancée, Allison, last fall. It was my fault, though. I still think about the things I should have done differently."

Natalie shifted uncomfortably in her chair. "How did your parents take the news of Harriet's death?"

"Dad was furious. He's only got one emotional response to anything, and that's anger. My mother will use Harriet's death to go on another drinking binge. By the way, I'm not close to either of them," he added with a frown.

"But you were close to Harriet?"

Ron shrugged. "Not until recently. My grandfather was always the important person in my life." His gaze shifted up, to the left, as if remembering a scene from the past. His face softened, like a child's. "Grandpa was a harsh guy. He would fly into a rage without any warning. But he always made me feel special, loved. A day with him would make up for a month with my parents." He looked back at Natalie. "I was crushed when he died. I still miss him."

Natalie felt the wine taking over, realized how exhausted she felt. She yawned and rose to put her glass in the sink. Ron said good night in the hallway and left, somewhat to Natalie's disappointment. She found an old blanket for Waldo, who pawed it into the correct position and curled up at the bottom of the staircase.

Waldo barked only once, late into the night. When she opened the bedroom window to listen, the smell of skunk filled the night air. In the distance a foghorn moaned a warning to ships nearing the jetty. The beacon from the coast guard station on the north spit sliced the fog with a single beam of light. She curled up beneath the blankets, clutching a pillow, feeling alone and frightened.

Should she stay? If she found the will, wouldn't she be in danger? Yet, if she left, Harriet's dream might never come to pass. Natalie's fear for herself was replaced by another fear: the thought of bulldozers clearing grassland next to the bay, birds fleeing in terror. Harriet's letter seemed to say the will had been hidden in such a way that Natalie was sure to find it. It would "surface." Finding the will might also flush out Harriet's murderer.

Natalie would stay.

Chapter Four: Helen

Natalie woke to the smell of coffee and bacon wafting up from the kitchen, and for a moment she thought Harriet was cooking breakfast. Then she remembered what had happened the day before. She dressed quickly in jeans and a cotton sweater, splashed cold water on her face and hurried downstairs. In the kitchen, Theresa was setting the table. Ron stood over the oven, flipping a pancake.

"Morning," he said. "I came up and got Waldo earlier so he wouldn't wake you. Helen will be here any minute. Deputies and dogs are searching the property for evidence, but they haven't found anything yet." Black circles under his eyes made Natalie wonder if he'd been awake all night.

The kitchen was usually the most cheerful room in the house. White curtains framed the tall windows. Pale yellow cupboards reached to the ceiling. The copper teapot whistled from a white enamel stove with red knobs. Yet the room seemed gloomy this morning.

Theresa handed Natalie a cup of coffee.

Ron sat down with a plate of pancakes, then helped himself to bacon and eggs from covered dishes on the table. "Have you eaten?" he asked, turning to Theresa.

"Hours ago. We get up at five-thirty to milk the cows."

As he turned back to eat, the girl studied him with unmistakable longing. So that's why Theresa is here, though Natalie, and she felt oddly jealous. Ron seemed unaware of the young girl's feelings.

A car drove up to the house. Theresa stood on tiptoes to peer out the window above the sink.

"It's Helen," she said.

Ron stopped eating, fork poised in midair, and frowned. "Don't be fooled by Helen's awful personality, Natalie. Deep down, she's really much worse than that. Right, Theresa?"

Theresa smiled, but didn't answer. Ron continued, "She does accounting in San Francisco, lives with another woman. Not that there's anything wrong with that, of course. Being gay, I mean, not accounting. There's plenty wrong with being an accountant." Ron snorted in amusement at his own joke and resumed eating. "She won't stay here," he said between bites. "Thinks this place is primitive, but I'm sure she knows how much it's worth."

The front door slammed, and Natalie heard the click of high heels on the wood floor of the hallway. Helen Frazier swept into the room, sleek and fashionable. Everything about her subtly signaled wealth, from the silk blouse to the stylish blunt cut of her auburn hair. Her face was a younger version of Harriet's, although more aristocratic, cold. Natalie caught a whiff of perfume as Helen pulled out a chair and sat down.

"Good morning, Ron," she said, her voice direct and businesslike. "I'll have coffee, Theresa." She pulled off her leather driving gloves, ignoring Natalie. "I spoke with the investigating detective—had to call him out of bed this morning from my car phone. They have no idea who killed Harriet. Not a single suspect. He says she was killed because she planned to change the will, give the farm to some nature group?" She crossed her legs and flicked a crumb from the corner of the table with her gloves.

Theresa placed a cup of coffee in front of Helen and turned away.

"Helen, this is Natalie Hughes," said Ron. "She's a wildlife biologist, and she's staying here. Natalie was with me when I found the body."

Helen made a gesture of acknowledgement toward Natalie, took a sip of coffee, then picked up a fork and began tapping it on the table. "I can't stay for more than a few days. The funeral will most likely be tomorrow. I spoke with the family attorney, and he will read the will to the family tomorrow evening. That should tie things up."

Ron put down his fork, wiped his mouth, and turned to Helen with a look of savage disapproval. "I don't know how you can be so cold when we're talking about your own mother."

Helen snorted. "We weren't exactly close, Ronnie. I'm sure you remember how they treated me when I—when I told them about Anne."

"I remember that you weren't very understanding."

"Understanding? That's right, I should have understood why dad stopped talking to me and mom couldn't leave me alone," snapped Helen. She put the fork down and lined it up neatly next to the plate. "At least it got me out of this backwoods dump. What have you been doing lately? Getting another degree?"

"I'm working on a dig in the ravine. Native artifacts."

"Dad cleared it all out years ago. The dining room has cases full of that stuff, along with all the other junk he collected."

Ron's face tensed, his eyes narrowed. "I have reason to believe there's more," he said, taking a sip of coffee and meeting Helen's stare.

Helen raised her eyes to the ceiling and sighed.

"Can I tell her about the letter?" Ron asked Natalie.

"If you want to," Natalie said with surprise, unsure what Ron meant by it.

Ron leaned across the table toward Helen, a calculating gleam in his eyes. "Harriet left a letter saying she'd written a new will and hidden it. She planned to give the farm to the Nature Conservancy for a wildlife refuge and sell the rest to the Wiyot tribe."

Helen slammed the coffee cup back on the table. "She was mad. Where's the letter?"

Ron sat back, smiling. He'd scored a hit.

"I'll get it," Natalie said. She could hear their raised voices all the way to her room upstairs, but they grew silent when she returned.

Helen snatched the letter from Natalie's outstretched hand and read it quickly. "I'd like to keep this," Helen said. "I want to have the handwriting examined."

"The letter belongs to Natalie, Helen."

Helen threw the letter on the table in front of Natalie. "Someone could have forged it. If a new will turns up, I'll be sure to have the handwriting examined."

Theresa, listening by the sink, suddenly looked alarmed. "If Harriet's farm becomes a wildlife refuge, we won't have enough pasture for our cattle," she said. "And the land those Indians want to buy is across from our house."

"That's right," Ron answered.

"I saw that old Indian, Henry Fishhawk, around lunch time yesterday, driving down the lane toward Harriet's place. What if he had something to do with... what happened?"

"Tell the sheriff," Helen said. "Fishhawk could be a suspect. Has anyone looked for the new will?" Helen turned her gaze from Ron to Natalie.

"We planned to search this morning," Natalie said.

"You don't need to worry, Helen. When we find it, you'll be the first to know," Ron said, leaning back in his chair and clearly relishing Helen's discomfort.

Helen glared at him and pushed her chair back from the table. "If it does turn up, you can be sure your father and I will contest it."

“It would almost be worth it to see you and Dad agree on something,” Ron said calmly.

Helen's gaze narrowed. Her cheeks reddened with anger. She stood up and stalked out of the house.

Chapter Five: Richard

Ron knelt near a pile of books in the study of the old Victorian. Natalie sat on an overstuffed sofa opposite him, several stacks of faded, musty-smelling books in front of her on a mahogany coffee table. She picked up one final book from the floor, thumbed through it and added it to the pile. “That's my last one.”

“I never thought it would be here,” Ron said, looking up at her. “But if she was in a hurry, this would be a likely place to hide the will.”

A horn honked in the driveway.

“Mom and Dad,” he said, wearily. “Ready to meet them?

Natalie nodded, picked up a stack of books and slid them back onto a shelf near the fireplace. The front door closed, and Natalie heard footsteps enter the living room. She followed Ron as he stepped into the other room.

Richard, a heavyset man in an expensive suit, puffed on a cigarette and exhaled the smoke through his nostrils, as if he could drain the tension from his face in a single release. Sheila, his wife, had opened the glass china cabinet to examine the contents. The sheriff's tape had been removed, and someone had draped a towel over the blood-stained upholstery where Harriet's body had lain the day before. There was still a spot on the floor.

Ron received a perfunctory hug from his father, a nod from his mother. Nobody seemed to want to sit down.

Richard muttered to his son, "I can't believe she's gone." He stubbed out his cigarette on an antique ashtray and rubbed his forehead. He had bushy graying hair and a long narrow nose like Ron's. Richard might have once been handsome, but now his face was creased with stress, and his eyes were those of a man who smothered emotion with thought.

"This is Natalie Hughes, Dad. She was friends with Harriet, and she's staying here while working at the refuge. Harriet left a letter for her about a new will."

Richard stared at his son with surprise. "She wrote a new will?"

"And hid it. We don't know where it is."

"You have the letter?"

Natalie pulled the note from her pants pocket, handed it to Richard. He put on a pair of reading glasses, studied the letter intently, then handed it back to her. His face showed no expression.

"I thought she was just teasing all those years, talking about deeding the land as a refuge." He fumbled in his pocket for another cigarette.

"Be careful of your blood pressure, Richard. You just finished a cigarette," Sheila said in a childish tone. She was an attractive woman, with dark hair like Ron's and hazel eyes, but she seemed too thin, her clothes too loose around her shoulders. A short haircut made her face look narrow, almost gaunt.

"Does Helen know about this?" Richard asked.

Ron nodded.

"Have you looked for the will?"

"I told you we haven't found it. We've already checked the bookshelves in the living room. The dining room is next. We're going to work our way up to the attic, then start on the bungalow if it hasn't turned up."

"Mother really was getting senile," Richard said. "She forgot things—appointments, birthdays."

"She didn't forget your birthday once, Richard," his wife admonished.

"No, she forgot her own. I called her on her birthday and she had completely forgotten what day it was."

"That hardly proves senility," Ron said.

"If it comes down to that, if this new will turns up, we may have to prove it. I'm counting on you to back me up, Ron," his father said sternly.

Ron looked into his father's eyes, opened his mouth to say something, then looked away. There was an awkward moment of silence.

"Natalie saw an intruder in here last night," Ron said. "They'd been looking through the study."

"They took a chapter of Harriet's memoirs," Natalie added. "Whoever broke in was on foot."

"It might be a good idea to take the valuables," Sheila said. "They might come back. I have a box in the car I could use to pack the china."

"Not now, Sheila," Richard said sharply, not looking at her. "I'll make sure the house is locked. We have to go to town and arrange the memorial."

"But Richard," Sheila whined, close to tears, "Harriet said I could have the china and silver. Helen will take everything."

"She will if she finds you started it first, Sheila," Richard snapped. "Leave it be."

Sheila turned and walked out the door. Richard followed. At the door he turned and looked at Ron. "If you need anything, let me know. Are you staying here a while?"

"I want to find the will before someone else does."

"Good. We want to keep this in the family." He smiled momentarily, then paused and looked around the room. He picked up a Hummel figurine from a lamp table near the door, a young boy petting a dog, and stared at it nostalgically. "I gave this to Mother for her birthday when I was ten."

Natalie felt a deep sense of sympathy for Harriet's only son. Harriet had told her of Richard's constant struggle to please Nathan, an intolerant, perfectionist father. Natalie recalled Harriet's face, full of pain as she told a story of Richard beaten because he had left a saw out in the rain.

Richard cleared his throat, looked up at Natalie. She wondered if he had somehow read her thoughts.

"Did you know my mother very well, Miss Hughes?" Richard asked. His tone was businesslike, but Natalie could see he was struggling to keep his composure.

"She was a good friend."

"Did she ever confide in you? I mean, did she ever say anything to you about our family?"

Natalie paused before answering, choosing her words carefully. "She said once that she wished she had been a better mother, but by the time she had learned from her mistakes it was too late. I know she loved you, Mr. Frazier."

"I'll never really know for sure, will I?" He put the figurine down, turned, and walked out of the house. Natalie heard their car pull away.

Natalie looked at Ron. "Are they always like this?"

"Pretty much. My time with Grandpa and Grandma was the only normal part of my childhood. Mom would always come and whisk me away just as I was starting to feel happy." Ron shrugged. "Guess that's why I came back this summer. Things weren't working, and I needed some space so I didn't snap." He turned away and stared out the window.

Natalie remembered something that Harriet had mentioned about Ron's summer visits, how he had always been a collector. Rocks, butterflies, seashells, whatever he found on his rambles around the farm was added to the collections in his room.

Natalie was startled by a knock at the door. Buck Davis peered in at her.

"We searched the area. No murder weapon. Whoever killed Mrs. Frazier must have taken it with them," Davis said as Natalie and Ron stepped outside to join him.

Davis put his hands in his pockets, head tilted up, looking down his nose, studying them with kind dark eyes, a polite smile on his face. He wore a gray suit that looked more comfortable than fashionable and a light blue shirt with no tie. His soft voice and gentle eyes made Natalie think of a priest.

She took the letter from her pocket and handed it to him. He held it out from his face, finding the focus point, then arched his eyebrows as he read. Ron fidgeted nervously, glancing at Davis and back away again.

"Well, this makes things a lot more interesting." He folded the letter and handed it back to her. "I didn't expect to find you here this morning, Miss Hughes."

"I've decided to stay," she said.

Davis looked her steadily in the eye. His face grew stern. He started to say something, stopped, rubbed his chin with one hand. "Might I have a word alone with you, Miss Hughes?"

"Sure," Natalie said.

Davis turned to Ron. "Would you excuse us?"

Ron looked annyoed, but nodded. Davis took Natalie gently by the arm and led her inside the Victorian, then closed the door behind them.

"Is there a reason Ron can't come?" Natalie asked.

"We don't like to discuss details of the investigation with possible suspects."

Chapter Six: Display Case

"Ron's a suspect?" Natalie asked, surprised at the anger in her own voice.

Davis touched her arm reassuringly and led the way into the formal dining room. A glass vase filled with drooping coral roses sat on a heavy oak table littered with petals. The heady scent of the rose filled the room. Glass display cases and china cabinets full of native artifacts lined the walls.

"I was poking around in here this morning," Davis said, motioning to the cases. "Pretty impressive. Like a museum."

"Harriet's husband was a collector." Natalie joined Davis next to a display case that held horn and bone utensils. Two carved spoons were labeled, *Elk horn spoons, Yurok, 1850*. Next to the spoons were obsidian arrowheads, chert scrapers and bone needles from various tribes in the area. There was an empty space on the bottom shelf, the shape of an instrument neatly outlined on the faded paper beneath.

"What belongs here?" Davis asked.

"A stone adze."

"Can you describe it?"

"The handle was made of gray stone, maybe sandstone. It was tapered at the end. The blade was a piece of chipped obsidian, about the size of my fist, tied to the handle with a strip of leather. The natives used them to make redwood slabs." Natalie glanced over at Davis. "Do you think it was the murder weapon?"

"It fits the description, and it gives us an idea of what to look for. If it was the murder weapon, the killer knew the house fairly well. Maybe he didn't intend murder when he came to see Harriet. I found something else that's interesting." He walked over to a glass cabinet and took out a piece of pottery with an intricate pattern of lines. "I didn't know the Indians around here made pottery." He handed it to Natalie.

"They didn't, but there was a lot of trading. This looks Southwest." The inside of the pot was decorated with black lines on a white background, a pattern of steps around the middle. The outside was painted in red adorned with a simple white zigzag.

"And finally, there's this." He opened the top drawer of the buffet, took out an envelope, showed her the color photographs inside. The first photo was a snapshot of a younger Harriet standing next to a dark-haired man.

"This is Harriet and Nathan," Natalie said. Adobe cliff dwellings clung to orange sandstone walls in the background. In another photo, Harriet stood beside a car, holding a pot resembling the one now sitting on the table. A fourth photo showed a matching pot in a display case with the label *Anasazi—1200 to 1450 A.D. Piñon Canyon.*

"This pot must be a replica," she said.

"Then how do you explain this?" He took a basket out of the case and handed it to her. It had a design similar to the pot, the red replaced with tan, the lines black.

"This is bear grass. The Wiyots used it. But this type of design was used all over the West—I don't see what it would prove."

"Would it be this exact?"

The basket had a tag: *Schooner Bluff, 1850*.

"I don't know," Natalie said.

Davis handed her a photo of a museum. A name was written on the back: *Max Ravenscroft, Curator, Santa Fe Museum of Natural History*. Beside it was a phone number.

"What do you think it means?" Natalie asked.

"I don't know what it means, but I'm going to find out."

He walked into the hallway, picked up the phone and dialed a number. A few seconds later he put down the receiver. "Got a shoe store."

He thumbed through the phone book, dialed again, asked for a number for the Museum of Natural History. He asked for Max Ravenscroft, nodded his head, put the receiver down. "They've never heard of him."

"The name does sound familiar. My ex-husband was an archeologist, and I spent some time looking through his books. I'm pretty sure I've seen that name in one of them. Let me do some research, see if I can locate this guy, and get back to you."

"Fine, if you want to try."

"It's funny, but I never noticed that pot. Harriet must have put it there recently. I'm sure I would have seen it before."

"I wouldn't leave it out if it was mine. Earthquakes." He gave her a frightened look.

"Put it in the buffet. It should be safe in the linens."

"Right." Davis shifted his weight uncertainly, as though he wasn't quite sure what a buffet without food might look like.

Natalie went to the buffet, opened drawers until she found one with napkins and tablecloths, and put the pot inside. "If anyone asks, I'll tell them it's here."

Davis had stopped in the hallway to examine a bear suit made from cloth and fur that stood beneath the staircase. The head was carved from wood, but the claws were real. "This one's pretty neat."

"Harriet didn't like it. She said it gave her goose bumps. I think her husband bought it from an old Kwakiutl in Vancouver who had worn it for ceremonies. Harriet thought it still had magic."

"You believe that stuff?" Davis stood in front of the suit and ran his fingers along the long claws hanging from fur-lined paws.

Natalie studied the head for a few minutes. It wasn't hard to imaging black eyes staring back at her from inside the mask. "I get a weird feeling when I look at it. I don't know what this costume was used for—probably just ceremonies to honor animal spirits. Bear shamans were considered very powerful. The local Indians didn't have bear shamans, but the Yuki farther south did. You know, the bear shaman's primary function was to seek out enemies of the tribe and kill them, usually when the tribe held a grudge against someone. The shaman would supposedly change into a bear before the kill." She shivered and rubbed her arms.

"Think I can get a deposition from him?" Davis asked with a grin.

He turned and saw Natalie's troubled expression, changed his tone.

"My wife would love it. She likes to scare herself, reads horror stories. Me, I see enough on the job." He rubbed his chin, fixed a steady gaze on Natalie. "I've been poking around here all morning. I like to get to know the victim—makes it more personal. I think I would have liked Harriet Frazier."

"I think you would have."

"Did you know she had cancer?"

"What?"

"We found a number of prescriptions for pain medication and sleeping pills in her medicine cabinet, all from an oncologist in Clam Beach. I called him this morning. Harriet Frazier had stomach cancer, with only a few months to live. Apparently she didn't tell anyone."

"She certainly didn't tell me." Natalie was gripped with a sense of anguish. Why had Harriet kept her illness a secret?

"Maybe she told someone in the family and they thought they couldn't wait a few months to inherit. Maybe her decision to deed the land away had something to do with knowing she was going to die, and she told the wrong person."

They walked outside together. Ron was nowhere to be seen.

"I can't offer you much protection if you stay," Davis said. "We've had cutbacks in the department. My own caseload has tripled, and I've got it easy compared with some." He handed her a card with his name and numbers for phone and beeper. "Call me if you find the will, or anything else that seems important. Don't tell anyone if you think you know where the will may be hidden, understand? Not even Ron Frazier. Who has keys to the place?"

"Lots of people. There was a plaque in the hallway with keys for the guests. I think Theresa Bergstrom has one, probably Ron."

"Do you have a gun?"

Natalie shuddered. "I hate the things, but I keep a baseball bat in my van. I used to play."

Davis started to grin as though she were joking, then realized she wasn't. "Just make sure you lock up at night."

"Ron's been leaving his dog with me."

"That's something," he muttered. "Keep in touch." He turned and strolled across the gravel drive to his car.

The Fraziers' car was gone, and so was Ron. Natalie stood for a long time, thinking about the implications of Harriet's illness. It would explain why so few guests had arrived in the past two weeks, explain why Harriet had seemed to be fading like the paper that lined her display cases. Now she was gone, leaving only a faint impression in the place she used to be, a space defined by the absence of what it once held.

Natalie walked up to her room and dialed a friend who owned a bookstore in the Bay Area.

"Marina Books. Good Morning."

"Paula? Natalie Hughes."

"Nat! How's life in the sticks?"

"I'll tell you some other time. Listen, does the name Max Ravenscroft ring a bell?"

"Sounds like the name of a villain in a cheap paperback."

"Look it up, will you?"

"Sure. Just a second."

There was a long pause.

"Here it is. Looks like he wrote several books about Southwest Indian tribes. One was illustrated. They're all out of print except the last—which was copyrighted in 1980. Nothing of his on the shelf."

"Thanks."

"Sorry I'm not much help. How do you like your job?"

"The job's fine. Everything else is awful. I'll call you when it gets better."

Natalie dialed the number of the museum in Santa Fe that Davis had written down. A receptionist answered.

"I'd like to speak to the head curator, please," asked Natalie.

"He's out right now. Can I take a message?"

“Can I speak to one of the regular staff? I have a question about an artifact that belongs to a friend. I think someone at your museum may have appraised it a few years ago.”

The line rang several times before someone picked it up at the other end. “This is Cheryl Santos.”

“My name is Natalie Hughes. I'm trying to locate Max Ravenscroft.”

“He hasn't worked here for years.”

“Is there anyone who might know how to reach him?”

“Not that I know of.”

“Would you mind asking?”

“Just a minute.” There was a rustle and a clunk as the phone was put down. “Stuart! Does anyone around here know where Max Ravenscroft lives now?” Pause. “He did? Okay. There's a woman on the phone trying to find him.” Rustle, rustle. “Hello? Hello?”

“Yes.”

“Our head curator got a Christmas card from him last year. Apparently Ravenloft lives somewhere around L.A.”

“Ravenscroft. Do you know where around L.A.?

“The curator would know.”

“Can I speak to him?”

“He’s gone for the afternoon.”

“Can I have his phone number?”

“I don’t think you’ll be able to reach him.”

Natalie held the phone out from her head and shook it for a second, then took a deep breath. "Can I leave a message, then? This is important."

"Um, I guess I can have him call you back. He'll be in tomorrow."

"Do you know when?"

"I don't know. Nine o'clock?"

"That would be eight o'clock my time. Thanks."

She left her number and hung up, then closed her eyes and sighed, feeling a mix of satisfaction and exasperation.

The house seemed suddenly close and heavy, pushing in on her with its many secrets. She imagined that's what it felt like wearing the bear costume—as if there might not be a way out once inside, as if a person might forget that they could take it off.

Chapter Seven: Henry

Outside Natalie's window, a heavy fog lay over the horizon in a broad, gray band. The tide had gone out, leaving the mudflats of the bay gleaming in the late afternoon light. She changed into khaki walking shorts and a cotton shirt, then tied a windbreaker around her waist in case the fog rolled in before her return. She dropped her camera and binoculars into her backpack, then glanced in the mirror. Her hair needed a wash. Instead, she put on a faded Giants baseball cap, pulled her hair through the opening in back, stuck sunglasses in her pocket and went downstairs.

In the hallway, she paused, feeling torn, wanting to search for the will. Yet her day was dictated by the tides. She had to make her count when the mud flats were exposed at low tide, drawing shore birds inland to the bay. Usually Natalie started her count earlier in the day, and now there wasn't much time left before the tide returned.

On the back porch, she grabbed her long, double-bladed kayak paddle and a light life vest. She made sure the doors were locked before she left.

As she walked down the path to the bay, she thought about the Frazier family. Could Richard have killed his own mother out of greed, knowing she was already dying? Then there was Helen—Ron was right about her. Cold and calculating. Capable of murder? It seemed more likely, given the personalities of Harriet's two children, that if one of them was that desperate they would hire someone to eliminate

Harriet and be sure to establish an alibi. Still, it was hard to believe either of them would commit matricide. Natalie wanted to believe it was someone else. Someone with a different motive. What had Davis said about his suspicions regarding Ron? Natalie shook her head—it wasn't worth thinking about.

The kayak was upside down where she had left it, a ten-foot, two-person fiberglass kayak on loan from the Department of Fish and Wildlife. It was flat bottomed, perfect for shallows, and could easily float in six inches of water or less. Natalie loaded her gear, pushed the kayak into the slough, climbed carefully in, and shoved off.

She glided smoothly along through water the color of dark creamed coffee, to a point where the slough opened into the choppy waters of the gray-green bay. She made her way to two large islands, all that remained of a vast salt marsh that had been slowly drained over a hundred years. Sandpipers waded in shallow water along the mud flats skirting the marsh. A dowitcher prodded the wet sand, searching for tiny mollusks.

A flock of tiny peeps took flight, sailed and banked sharply showing a pattern of white undersides, then darted off across the bay. Behind the fog bank hovering offshore was another row of higher, darker clouds, limned with afternoon light. Natalie paddled along, trying to imagine how the birds perceived the bay—the glimmer of a fish under the water, the brush of wind and air currents, the chatter of other birds.

Natalie felt like a creature of the tides. The roar of pounding breakers a half mile away, where the ocean sent waves crashing against the jetty, drowned her thoughts in a soothing rhythm. What passed for civilization was only a dream, thought Natalie. This was the real world. In the past month she had spent more and more time here, savoring the solitude.

Today, she needed it more than ever. Harriet's death, her own grief, and the task of finding the will seemed overwhelming. Natalie sensed she was walking a tightrope. If she gave way to despair, depression was just around the corner, waiting like the stormclouds building up behind the fog.

She closed her eyes, opened herself to the sounds and smells of the bay, felt the lapping of small waves against the kayak, the soft breeze against her cheeks, listened to the cries of seagulls overhead.

She thought of Harriet's commitment to the land and her own love for the older woman. Natalie's eyes filled with tears. It had taken Harriet most of her long life, and a difficult struggle, but she had overcome the values learned in her childhood and discovered her own. The new will embodied those values, values Natalie shared.

She took a deep breath, wiped her eyes. If Harriet had chosen Natalie to find the will and set things straight, then Harriet knew Natalie had the strength and courage to do it. Beneath the anguish and despair, Natalie found resolution and determination. As she paddled back toward the bluff and Harriet's farm, it was with a sense of purpose and certainty that she would prevail.

Two brown pelicans flew low over the water, laboriously flapping their huge wings. She followed them with the binoculars until they reached deeper water at the mouth of the bay. Sighting fish, they turned and, one at a time, folded their wings like collapsing umbrellas to plummet into the bay, showering spray above them. They surfaced and bobbed on the waves, gular pouches open to release the water so they could swallow their catch.

The tide was coming back in, and Natalie rode it back up the slough, paddling gently. She pulled out the kayak and climbed to Spirit Rock, sat munching an apple. From her vantage point she could see many miles in every direction. It was a place where the edges of separate worlds met and merged. The bay was protected on the west by a spit that stretched north for several miles, bordered by the white foam of breakers like a profile of lace. Here and there, giant driftwood sculptures of redwood stumps lay half buried in sand, their wood bleached and smoothed by wind and sea. They had journeyed from inland forests, carried down churning rivers during seasonal floods, washed ashore by the crashing waves of winter storms. The fog was rolling in now, sweeping over the spit like a great wave.

To the east lay ascending hills with mysterious ravines, where the tall spires of sitka spruce rocketed upward, reaching into the sky.

There, she knew, sparkling creeks ran clear and cold, and the smell of salt air mixed with the pungent odor of

spruce needles.

Far away to the north on the misty horizon, the rooftops and smokestacks of Clam Beach skirted the harbor where sailboats tacked in the breeze. Long ago the edges of two civilizations had met here. One had conquered, the other nearly vanished.

South of the point where she sat, a river merged with the ocean, pouring fresh water into salt. It was impossible to tell where river ended and sea began. Farms were edged with land still wild and untamed, too steep to plow or log. Natalie thought of the foxes and weasels, skunks and raccoons, the bobcats that made their homes there on the fringe of cultivated land and human habitation.

She dozed, leaning against the rock. She opened her eyes when the wind picked up, blowing her hair back from her face, turning her cheeks cold. Wet fog blew past in long streamers, cloaking the bluff and the bay. She pulled on her windbreaker, put on her cap, and sat hugging her knees, grateful for the sun-warmed rock against her back.

The sound of a footstep startled her. She jumped up, turned around. For a moment she thought the figure she saw was a trick of the mist and rocks. An old Indian stood silently several yards away. Then he walked toward her and held out a hand.

Chapter Eight: Medicine Bird

"Hello. I'm Henry. You must be Nat. Harriet told me about you."

She heaved a sigh of relief and grasped his outstretched hand. It was rough and wrinkled, calloused on the palm. His look was direct, piercing yet warm. His long, gray hair was drawn back in a ponytail. He wore a faded checkered flannel shirt over a white T-shirt and jeans.

"I saw Harriet yesterday," he said. "I'd just got back after being gone for a while. She asked me to witness her will, said if anything happened to her I should find you. I thought she was talking crazy. Then I found out she'd been killed."

"How did you know where to find me?"

"I saw you beach the kayak beside the slough. I checked at the house but no one was there, so I thought I'd walk out to the big rock. I come here sometimes to pray. It's a popular spot."

"I've always been drawn to rocks. Especially big ones like these."

"There's a reason for that." Henry walked over to the rocks and sat down on a flat place. "Rocks have memories. Some carry messages from our ancestors, but only if you are able to listen." He ran one hand over the rough surface of the rock, almost in a caress. "I don't get why the ancient people in Europe hauled the rocks for miles and put them in circles. Why would you do that if the rocks had already arranged themselves?" He glanced up at Natalie, as if watching for her reaction.

Natalie thought of the book Harriet had left, the letter. It wasn't a coincidence she had picked this place.

"Harriet hid the will somewhere," Natalie said. "Did you read it before you signed it?"

"Yes."

Her stomach tightened. "What did it say?"

He paused a moment, studying her face. "It gave all the bottom land to the Nature Conservancy, but with no more grazing or hunting. They hunt over on the refuge, and she didn't like it. Said you'd told her some of the duck populations were way down, and the best breeders were getting shot."

"What about the rest?"

"Sixty acres go to the tribe. The sale's in escrow right now—we were going to sign the papers next week. And we get her collection of artifacts back."

"And the family?"

"They get the houses and ten acres around it up on the bluff. She said it was enough. At least three hundred thousand, with the view."

"Had anyone else signed the will when you saw it?"

"No."

"You were there around eleven o'clock?"

"How did you know?"

"Theresa Bergstrom saw you drive past their place. Has Detective Davis talked to you?"

Henry glanced quickly away and stared out at the ocean.

“No,” he said. “I wanted to find out what Harriet's letter said before I talked to the sheriff. I heard about the letter at the store. Carol Bergstrom was in, spreading gossip like always.”

“News travels fast around here,” Natalie said. She explained the contents of the letter as Henry listened, his face impassive, still staring out over the ocean.

“Harriet seemed worried when I saw her,” Henry said. “I asked if anything was wrong, but she said she wasn't sure. She didn't want to talk about it. She was expecting an old friend for lunch, a Mr. Duffy.”

“Detective Davis is going to question him. She had cancer, you know.”

“She didn’t tell me. She was a strong woman.”

Natalie sat on the grass the edge of the rock and plucked a tiny coral scarlet pimpernel. “Henry, do you know what willow bark is used for?”

“We use it to make a tea for chronic pain. It has other uses, like helping seedlings grow.”

“You didn't happen to give some to Harriet the day she died, did you? I found a jar of green bark on the windowsill in the kitchen.”

“No. Check with Mary Slocum. She's the local herbalist. Her grandmother was Yurok. You can find her if you drive along the road—she picks up trash each day.”

“Is she the one who wears bright clothes and a red baseball cap?”

"That's her."

"Mary might have been there yesterday. If so, she could have seen someone. I was out on the bay all afternoon, working. Henry, I think Harriet was killed by someone who knew her."

"You take bird counts, right?"

"For Fish and Wildlife. It's a big project, mostly with volunteers, but they need an accurate count at the refuge."

He laughed. "White people are so weird. Always counting things to see if a place is healthy." He looked at her and saw her expression, looked away. "Sorry. I'm just a cynical old Indian. I like birds, though."

"So do I. Maybe counting them isn't the best way to help, but it's a start."

"My family name comes from the osprey, the fish hawk. It's our medicine bird. It was endangered, but now it's coming back, like us Indians." He grinned teasingly. "Do you have a medicine bird?"

"I hadn't really thought about it." Her gaze wandered to the ocean. "I suppose it would be the brown pelican. I wish I could lift up and fly with them whenever I see a line of pelicans go by. Is that medicine?"

"Absolutely. Whatever brings you back to your connection to the earth, to your true spirit." He chuckled. "Steinbeck wrote that pelicans always seem to know exactly where they're going."

She laughed. "Well, that's what I need in my life right now. A sense of direction. I don't think I can live in the city any more, but I'm not sure where I belong." She dropped the coral scarlet pimpernel back in the grass and tried to wipe the flower's stain from her hands, but it had dyed her skin too deeply. "I thought the Indians didn't want white people to use their medicine. I try to avoid that sort of thing."

"Good. A lot of white people want to become Indians. They follow spiritual leaders, do sweats, simple bullshit like that. They want a quick fix for what's wrong with them. A lot of my people are really bitter about it, you know, because the whites took our land and forced Christianity on us. And now they're trying to steal our religion, too, because theirs doesn't work for them anymore. But I don't think that way."

He looked at the crashing waves below and rubbed his chin, then back at her to see if she was still listening. Natalie wasn't sure what to say.

Henry pointed to the bay, partially hidden by fog. "The highest population of whites in this part of California lives on land that once belonged to my people, the Wiyot. My ancestors lived all around the bay and on the islands." His voice softened, and his eyes grew dreamy. "We were still water people. Other tribes lived along the rivers or near the ocean, but the bay was ours." He turned to her, held her gaze. His eyes seemed to reflect deep pools of sadness. "In 1860 my people were meeting for a ceremony on one of the islands when a group of white men massacred them in their sleep. It was all very systematic. Axes and hammers so there wouldn't be any gunshots to wake the rest. They almost wiped us out."

He picked up a pebble, weighed it in his hand as if about to throw it, then dropped it back onto the rock. "I've thought about the racial problems a long time," Henry said. "The whites came over here looking for land because Europe was overpopulated. They had to divide up their land and fight over it. It made them greedy and heartless, but maybe they couldn't help it. They lost their connection to what's important. A lot of the Indians lost that too, but we only lost it a hundred years ago, not a thousand.

"So I don't really mind if the white man uses our medicine to find his soul, if it works, but I'm not so sure it does. I think he has to invent a new religion, a new way of being that combines our ways and his knowledge. I don't know how this can be done, but someone has to start. You can count all the birds you want, but what this bay needs is to just be left alone so she can heal herself. And that's basically what the birds need. Not a lot of netting, and banding, and counting."

He stood and brushed off his pants.

Natalie bristled at the insult. She stood, took a deep breath, and stared at Henry. "I understand what you're saying, Henry. I feel the same way. Lots of biologists do, but the people in power only understand statistics, because they make the important decisions from offices, so that's the only way we have to prove what needs to be done. Maybe I have to dance with the devil, but I'm willing to do it to get things done."

Henry smiled at Natalie and clapped his hand on her shoulder. "Now I know why Harriet liked you so much. Watch out for the Bergstroms, Natalie. Harriet had something on them. Something she wouldn't tell me, 'cause she probably knew I'd just turn right around and tell everyone."

"I'm starting to think I should pay them a visit," said Natalie. "Theresa trusts me. Jack always waves to me on the road, and I haven't even met him. Maybe they'll talk to me."

"Jack'll play the friendly cowpoke only so long as you don't cross him. He's meaner than a skunk and twice as cunning. Be careful."

Henry turned and walked stiffly away, limping slightly.

Natalie thought about the skunk that had wiped out Harriet's small flock of chickens. They found the bloody carcasses in the morning, all with their heads missing. If Jack Bergstrom was going to be an adversary, she wanted to meet him first on his home ground, size him up before he came looking for her.

Chapter Nine: Bergstrom

When Natalie came downstairs early the next morning, the house was empty. Ron had arrived after dinner the night before, and they had spent the evening searching for the will. When they had finally given up it was nearly midnight. He had left Waldo with her, but now the dog was gone. Ron must have risen early and come to the house to let Waldo out.

Natalie peered glumly into the refrigerator, pulled out a half-gallon of milk, smelled it, and emptied it into the sink. The remains of last night's enchilada casserole looked unappetizing, but the vegetable compartment held mushrooms, zucchini and an end of Monterey Jack cheese. An omelet would taste good. An empty egg carton on the bottom shelf gave her an idea.

Carol Bergstrom sold fresh eggs. It was an innocent excuse to meet Theresa's parents, and a good time of day to find them at home. First she needed to wake up. Natalie brewed coffee, burned her mouth slurping it. She added cold water, which made it tepid. The day was not off to a good start.

There was a clopping of hooves outside. Peering out the window, Natalie saw Theresa going through the pasture gate on her horse. The young girl carried something in a feedbag, the top part wrapped around the saddle horn. She watched as Theresa dismounted and turned to close the gate. The girl looked upset, wiping her cheeks with the back of her hand as she climbed back on the horse and headed toward Ron's camp. Maybe she was taking him supplies. But why the tears? A fight with her parents?

A few minutes later, Natalie climbed into her van and turned the key. Nothing happened. The knob for the headlights was pulled out, probably from a few days earlier when she had driven through fog in the late afternoon.

Harriet's white Ford was parked in the tiny garage, but the keys were missing. A pair of ancient bicycles leaned against the wall, but the tires were flat. It took twenty minutes to locate a rusty pump and inflate them. Riding a bicycle for the first time in years made Natalie feel like a little girl. She hoped the tires had lost their pressure over time, and not from a puncture.

Jack Bergstrom's red pickup and horse trailer were parked in the farmyard by the side of his huge white barn. A buckskin mare stood tethered to a hitching post, her tail switching flies, a dark patch of sweat on her back from where a saddle had been removed.

A border collie and Australian shepherd lying near the barn door stood up and barked. Natalie stopped the bicycle, put out one leg for balance, and nearly fell over. She waited uncomfortably for someone to appear. The collie, which seemed to take his job seriously, ran forward a few steps and bared his teeth. The shepherd merely wagged his tail as her stared at Natalie from one blue and one brown eye.

Jack Bergstrom stuck his head out of the barn door.

"Shep! Bart! Com'ere!"

The dogs ran back to him and lay down at his feet. He said something else in a low voice. They jumped into the bed of the pickup and sat waiting. Bergstrom took off his cowboy hat, wiped his brow with one hand, and nodded to Natalie as she lay the bike down on the grass and walked over.

"Mornin' to you, Miss Hughes. What can I do for you?" A big man, with a tanned face and blonde hair cut short, he smiled widely at her, showing his teeth. His eyes were intense and direct. Someone who was used to being in control. Someone you wouldn't want to fool with.

"Morning. Theresa told me you sold eggs. I'd like to buy a dozen."

"Carol's in the house," Jack said, gesturing with his thumb. "She usually has some eggs, if she hasn't sold them already." He smiled broadly, with warmth that seemed genuine. There was something roughly attractive about him. If it hadn't been for Henry's warning, she knew she would have liked Jack Bergstrom immediately.

They both turned at the sound of hoof beats on the road. Theresa galloped in on her horse. She pulled up a few feet away and patted the young roan stallion on the neck. His nostrils flared and he danced in place, full of energy.

"Hi, Dad. Miss Hughes," she said, out of breath, her eyes sparkling with excitement. Not at all the distraught teenager Natalie had seen thirty minutes earlier. Theresa's long blonde hair was pulled back in a flattering ponytail. She wore a lime green jacket, tooled leather cowboy boots. With a surge of jealousy, Natalie realized how beautiful the girl was, and wondered what Ron thought of her.

"I thought I told you to stay off that colt 'til he was full broken in!" Jack said in feigned frustration.

Theresa swung down from the saddle and tied the colt next to the buckskin, which whinnied softly.

"I used a hackamore, Dad. He doesn't like a bit. That's why he's been so fussy. See, he's gentle as a lamb."

She took her father's arm. Natalie could see the closeness between them as his stern face softened and beamed with pride.

"She's a natural," he said. "Could probably run this place by herself."

"And will, someday," Theresa added.

"Don't get ahead of yourself—I'm not dead yet. For now, why don't you cool off that colt and brush him down."

Theresa loosened the girth on the saddle.

"I would have gone to town for groceries but my car won't start," Natalie said.

"What's wrong with it?" Jack asked.

"The battery's dead. I left the lights on."

"I can come over later and jump it for you. Are you going to the funeral?"

"Yes. Thanks for the jump. I should be back from the bay around one o'clock. The funeral starts at two."

"Sounds good." He turned and untied the quarter horse to lead it away. Natalie walked the bike to the back porch of the house. A Bard Rock rooster and some hens eyed her suspiciously, then resumed pecking and scratching around the flowerbeds.

Carol Bergstrom opened the door before Natalie knocked. She must have been watching from the kitchen. Carol had the pinched face of someone who sized people up with the intent of finding fault.

Harriet had spoken of Carol with a mixture of pity and disgust. "Everyone needs an antagonist in life," she once told Natalie. "It keeps one from becoming too complacent. I've learned to love hating Carol Bergstrom."

Stonewashed jeans and a mint green sweatshirt made Carol look younger than the lines on her face indicated. Her light hair was cut short, and she wore oversized glasses.

"Theresa said you might sell me some eggs. My car won't start, and I can't get to town."

"Come on in," Carol said. She turned and walked into the house.

Natalie stepped into a warm, sunny kitchen. Smelling freshly baked cinnamon rolls, she spied two dozen cooling on the counter next to the oven. Her mouth watered.

The farmhouse was old, but the kitchen looked recently remodeled, with new walnut cabinets. Copper kettles hung from an iron ring on the ceiling. Marching geese lined a wallpaper border on the wainscoting. A brick hearth framed a beautiful white enamel wood stove. The effect was charming. Carol had expensive taste.

Carol disappeared into a narrow pantry for a moment, then popped back out. "Theresa must have sold the last dozen yesterday. I'll go check the henhouse. Jack insists on having fresh eggs, but we have too many in the summer and not enough in the winter when they don't lay well."

After Carol left, Natalie glanced around the dining room. A huge rolltop desk stood in the corner. The temptation was too much. Natalie walked over and leafed through a stack of bills and letters that lay in a pile. Household bills. There was a box of floral stationery, various church bulletins, news clippings. It must have been Carol's desk. It felt completely out of character, but her sense of propriety had suddenly vanished. If someone wanted to hide something, like a stolen chapter from Harriet's memoirs, it wouldn't stand out among all the files and records in a desk. She opened drawers and searched the contents, stopping every few moments to listen for Carol. Just as she heard the chickens squawk she found an unmarked folder, opened it, and recognized Harriet's handwriting.

"I can still remember that evening when I found the burial cave with the beautiful pot."

Chapter Ten: Burial Site

Natalie quickly folded the pages and stuffed them into the back of her pants, pulling her shirt out to hide them. She tried to look politely bored, gazing out the window over the dining room table as Carol returned.

"You have a wonderful view of the bay," Natalie said.

"Thank you. I've got more than a dozen eggs here. How many do you want?"

"I'll take a carton."

Carol washed the eggs and placed them in a pink styrofoam egg carton. Natalie gave her a dollar, which Carol added to a jar of bills and change on the counter.

"I suppose you're going to the memorial service this afternoon?" Carol asked, wiping her hands on a towel.

"I plan to. The battery's dead in my car, but your husband offered to jump start it for me."

"Harriet was a good friend of mine, you know."

Natalie paused before answering. "She certainly spoke of you often."

"Theresa told us about the new will. I can't believe Harriet would deed the land to some environmental group. She knew it would hurt us. We'll have to send the cattle inland to pasture, and that'll cost. Didn't anyone witness the will?"

"Henry Fishhawk says he did."

"That old Indian? Why would Harriet trust him?"

"Because part of the land will be sold to the tribe."

Carol stiffened. Her eyes grew cold and still. She grabbed a paper towel and wiped fiercely at the counter. "I heard about that. If they get ahold of the bluff, land values will drop, that's for sure. They'll put a bunch of trailers up here and turn it into a junkyard. You know they don't have to follow county laws once they get ahold of a piece of land. Probably open a bingo parlor. We'll have all kinds of weird people driving by."

"I happen to like bingo, myself," Natalie said.

Carol shot her an icy stare.

Natalie moved toward the door. "I have to be going. Thank you for the eggs."

Carol nodded, lips pursed in anger, and opened the screen door. "We should all be careful. God knows what the murderer might still have planned."

Natalie pulled her shirt lower in back, afraid the folded papers might pop out when she got on the bike, and walked away without a word. She put the eggs in the wire basket, eased onto the seat, and pedaled away standing up.

Jack was by the barn, trying to coax one of the horses into the trailer. The horse balked. Jack cussed at it, took off his hat, and hit it on the rump. His face was red with rage. He slammed the tailgate closed and stormed into the barn.

As soon as she had returned to the Blue Heron, Natalie hurried into the kitchen, spread the missing diary pages on the table, and began to read:

"I thought little of that day for years, until my friend Duffy asked me in one of our regular chats when I first became interested in Indian artifacts...

"I believe I must have been three or four years old that summer, which would have been 1919 or 1920. My father, Mr. O'Neil, was head milker at the Frazier farm, and our family had been invited to an ice cream social at the 'big house'—what we called the Frazier's old Victorian in those days. When my mother forbade me from having thirds of ice cream, I wandered off in search of something interesting.

"I recall being led to the ravine by an old raven hopping about on the limbs of alders above. I thought he was calling me to follow, but he was probably just scolding. I had been warned against playing there, because the spring before a small child had drowned in a swollen creek. But the raven made me forget. I followed it down along the scree of rocks to the banks of the creek. The slope was much shallower then. Now it must be close to a thirty-foot drop.

"There was foxglove everywhere. I peeked inside each one, looking for fairies, and picked a few for my mother. I hoped a gift of flowers might save me from a spanking.

"Something made me look up. I believe it was the raven's warning call. On the edge of the ravine a bobcat stood staring at me. I don't know if it would have killed me, or if it was only trying to scare me away from its den, but I ran down the gully toward the ocean. I hid behind some thick bushes to rest for a moment, and saw there a cave in the cliff. The opening was only big enough for a small child, but inside it was larger. There was a pool of light in the cave where the sun shone through the opening, and in the middle of the light was a large box.

"Inside the box was a collection of pottery. One in particular caught my eye. Taking the pot, I placed the top back on the box. It was warm inside the cave, and I was tired from running. I lay down in the sun and must have fallen asleep.

"When I awoke, it was night. The moon shone directly into the cave, the light falling on something white in the back of the cave. It was a skeleton, curled up like a fetus. I screamed and crawled outside. Dark figures with lanterns moved above the ravine, calling to me. I don't know what happened to the pot. I think I may have left it near the entrance to the cave. At that point I was more afraid of my mother. She took me home, spanked me until I was sore, and sent me to bed without my dinner.

"Years later, Nathan found the pot half buried in clay at the bottom of a slide. We kept the pot for years, until a visiting archeologist told us the patterns were Anasazi. That led us to Max Ravenscroft, who identified it as identical to 500-year-old pottery from a Southwest dig.

"We kept our find a secret. Nathan thought people would call it a hoax without more proof. He looked for the cave from time to time, but never found a trace. The Wiyot baskets from this area have a similar pattern. Were they related? Are the Wiyot descended from a wandering group who survived the collapse of the Anasazi?

"Duffy and I walked the ravine, but the landscape has changed so much I haven't a clue where the cave is anymore. That's why I shared the secret with my grandson, in the hope he might be able to find the box."

Natalie put the pages down. This explained Ron's interest in the ravine. He was looking for something far more important than scrapers and bone needles. But why did Carol Bergstrom steal the chapter? Assuming it was Carol, and not Jack or Theresa.

If Carol thought Harriet possessed damaging information about the Bergstroms, Carol may have been looking for it when she stumbled onto the chapter about the pot. And if Carol knew Harriet was planning to sell land to the tribe, she would surely want to conceal any evidence of a burial cave, which would strengthen the Wiyot's case.

The phone rang, startling Natalie out of her reverie. She glanced at her watch. It was eight o'clock.

Chapter Eleven: Ravenscroft

"This is Dave Franklin. I'm calling for Natalie Hughes."

"Speaking. I'm trying to locate Max Ravenscroft."

"You a friend of his?"

"Good friends. Great friends, actually, but I've lost touch with him over the years. Just wanted to see how he's doing."

"Oh. Well, he moved somewhere around L.A., but I got a card from him last Christmas. Let me see if I still have it. Hang on a sec."

He put her on hold. She listened to Navajo flute music for several minutes. Finally, he picked up the receiver.

"Sorry. Can't find it anywhere. Must have thrown it out. I did write back to him, though. I remember addressing the card, thinking how nice the weather would be in Southern California in December."

"Do you remember what part of Los Angeles he lived in? A street address or something?" Ten million people lived "somewhere around L.A." Without an address her chances of finding Ravenscroft were slim to nil.

"Well, let me see. It wasn't really L.A. The postmark was L.A., but the address was something like Wellington Heights or, no, not Wellington… what's the name of the palace? Windsor! That's it. Windsor Hills."

Natalie breathed a sigh of relief. "I don't suppose you recall a street name." A moment of silence. Her heart was racing. Please remember.

"It was a food, like a salad food, you know. One of those California street names. Let me see."

"It's extremely important," she said.

"It wouldn't be avocado. Even Californians wouldn't name a street avocado. Olive! That's it. Olive Street. I bet it's lined with olive trees." Franklin sounded pleased with himself.

"Thank you, Mr. Franklin. You must have a great memory."

"No problem," he answered, obviously in a better humor than when he first made the call. "If you get ahold of him, tell him 'hi' for me. He must be about eighty by now. Nice guy. I learned a lot from old Max."

"He sounds like a nice man."

"I thought you said—"

"Thanks for your time!"

Natalie hung up, embarrassed by her mistake, but with a nervous fluttering in her stomach that said she was on the right rack.

She dialed information for Windsor Hills. There was a Max Ravenscroft on Olive Avenue. She listened to the phone ring, seven, eight, nine times. No answer.

As she was about to hang up, someone picked up the receiver.

"Hello?" A woman's voice, faint.

"I'd like to speak to Max Ravenscroft, please."

"One moment."

The moment seemed to take forever.

"Hello, this is Max Ravenscroft." The voice was old, raspy, but strong.

"Mr. Ravenscroft, my name is Natalie Hughes. I'm calling from Northern California, near Clam Beach."

"Never heard of it. What did you say your name was?"

"Natalie Hughes."

"If you're selling something, I'm not interested."

"No! No, I'm calling about a piece of Anasazi pottery I think you authenticated for a friend of mine."

Silence.

"Are you still there, Mr. Ravenscroft?"

"Yes, I'm here. What about it?"

"The pot belonged to a couple—the Fraziers. They visited you in Santa Fe back in the sixties."

"Lots of people have come to see me with pots, Miss Hughes. Hundreds. I don't remember them all."

"A photograph said the pot may have come from a place called Piñon Canyon. Does that ring a bell?"

"Piñon Canyon. Oh my, yes! I was on that dig. I must have been about thirty." His voice changed, the tone softened by nostalgia. "It was north of Santa Fe, up on the Ojo Caliente. Of course there are hundreds of sites, some of them still being found, but that one... that one was the most exciting for me. We were the first to find it. Got there ahead of the pot hunters."

He paused for a moment to cough, a wet, rattling sound. Natalie cringed.

"That pot," Ravenscroft said, his voice hoarse. He coughed again. "The one that couple had, it matched the one in the museum, but they were real secretive about where they'd gotten it. Personally, I didn't care where it came from. It would have helped to know for sure, but it didn't come from Piñon Canyon."

"How can you know for sure?"

"Piñon Canyon was abandoned around 1450. There weren't any signs of digging, or even footprints, when we first arrived. We found everything there was to find."

"So you're sure the Frazier pot was authentic?"

"Positive. It was a beautiful piece. I made them an offer. They said they'd think about it and come back the next day, but they never did. That pot would be worth a lot of money nowadays, especially on the black market."

"Mr. Ravenscroft, I have reason to believe they may have found the pot buried on their farm in Northern California."

There was a long pause on the other end. "This isn't some kind of hoax, is it?"

"I don't think so. They never told anyone about it. They probably thought no one would believe them unless they found more."

"That pot was at least five hundred years old. There was a lot of trading back and forth through various tribes, but that's a long way for one pot to travel."

"Thank you, Mr. Ravenscroft. You've been a big help."

He ignored her dismissal. "There was a theory, years back. No one paid much attention to it. Someone wrote a paper in Curator Quarterly, in the early seventies."

"What was the theory?"

"Well, the Algonkin language group has an unusual distribution in North America. Most of the tribes that spoke it were in the Northeast and Canada, like the Algonquin. But there's a little patch of it in the Southwest. The guy who wrote the article theorized that the Anasazi may have belonged to that language group, like the Navajo are. No one knows for sure. But there is one other place where the dialect was definitely Algonkin, and that's always been a mystery."

"Where?"

"Northern California. The Wiyot and Yurok tribes. Of course, those languages have become extinct in this century, so there's no way to know anymore."

She couldn't answer for a moment, her throat tight. "Mr. Ravenscroft, we found the pot in the area where the Wiyots once lived."

"You know, the Anasazi disappeared from New Mexico and Arizona between 1200 and l450. Nobody knows where they went, but someone might be able to trace the baskets. The early Anasazi were called 'the basket weavers' because they wove exquisite basketry, so fine it could hold water."

"The tribes around here are some of the finest basket makers in the country."

"This whole idea would be very hard to substantiate. One pot won't do it," he said.

"How could someone prove that the pot came from here?"

"You'd have to find more, or find the place where it came from, and see if there are any potsherds left. Then try to date the organic material found with it. It's pretty far-fetched. I'm inclined to think that pot made its way out there fairly recently, sometime in the past couple of hundred years."

"Mrs. Frazier found a burial cave when she was a child. The pot was with others in some kind of chest, or a box."

"The Anasazi didn't have chests."

"But the Wiyot did. Made from wood slabs."

"If you find that cave, Miss Hughes, I wish you'd call me. I'm somewhat infirm, but I'd fly up immediately. It would be a fantastic discovery, to prove that some of the Anasazi made it all the way to the coast. Imagine their joy, finding a world where water is a problem instead of a scarcity!"

"I promise you'll be the first to know, Mr. Ravenscroft."

"By the way, how is that couple?"

“I'm afraid they're both dead.”

“I'm sorry to hear that. They were very nice. I wish they had sold me that pot.”

Natalie said goodbye and put the receiver down. She wanted to touch the pot, examine it again. She opened the drawer to the buffet where she had hidden it. The linens were pushed aside, the pot gone.

Chapter Twelve: Inheritance

Harriet's family sat together in the living room of the Victorian after the memorial. Ron had asked Natalie to join them, and she stood near the window, sipping tea and feeling uncomfortable. It was late afternoon. A dense fog had drifted in from the coast, adding a chill to the air. She shivered and walked into the kitchen to refill her cup. When she returned, she stood near the hallway leading to the back rooms, waiting for the appropriate moment to excuse herself.

Helen and Richard were engaged in small talk, chatting with forced friendliness and frequent, awkward pauses. It seemed as though they were all trying to be a family, but not succeeding very well. Everyone had a separate agenda. Harriet was no longer there to hold them together, and Natalie sensed they would quickly drift apart.

"What are you going to do with the ashes, Dad?" Ron asked. He was sitting in a chair in the corner. "Harriet wanted them spread out at Spirit Rock, but this time of day the wind will likely blow them right back at you."

"I think I'll leave the urn here, and you can do it, Ron, if you don't mind," Richard said. "It would be too painful for me."

"I know Harriet would understand."

"Does anyone want more coffee?" Helen asked. No one answered, and she disappeared into the kitchen.

"I wish you'd speak to her about the china," Sheila said to Richard. "I'd like to take it today. Harriet said I could have it."

"Can't it wait, Sheila?"

"No. I want it now."

Sheila got up, took her purse, and went to the bathroom.

When Helen returned, Natalie set her cup down and cleared her throat. "I wanted to ask all of you if I might stay a few days longer. There really isn't any affordable place close to the bay during tourist season. My job will be over in a month, when the resident biologist comes back from maternity leave."

"And you need time to look for the phantom will, right?" Helen asked.

Natalie didn't answer.

"I talked to Wayne Baumeister, Harriet's attorney, this afternoon," Helen said. "Harriet's will was written years ago, and he has it safe. It leaves everything to the family. We can all go in tomorrow and discuss it with him."

Sheila brushed past Natalie on her way back from the bathroom, trailing the smell of scotch. Richard glanced at his wife with disgust.

"Harriet left me everything in the china cabinet," Sheila said.

"That remains to be seen," Helen replied, looking at Sheila with a mocking gleam in her eye. "Let's see what the will says."

"She left it to me!" Sheila's voice rose.

"It's true, Helen," Richard chimed in. "Harriet promised Sheila the china. She has a sentimental attachment to the old things in the house."

"Sentimental, my ass," Helen said. "That antique china is embossed with 24-karat gold."

Richard's face turned sour. "The point is, Helen, you never cared about Mom anyway."

Helen stood there a moment, looking like she had been struck. Then her eyes lit up with a fierce anger. She steadied herself and slowly put her cup down.

"Don't talk to me about love, Richard Frazier. What do you know about it? The lack of love was never on my side. I adored our parents when I was young. I did everything they asked, and it made me miserable. They only thing they cared about was whether I lived up to their expectations."

The others were silent. Richard stared uncomfortable at the carpet.

"They wanted us to be exactly like them," snapped Helen. "And you were. When I came out, when I was honest about my own feelings, all hell broke loose."

She looked around, her anger suddenly melting into an expression of yearning, like a child looking for comfort. She wiped tears from one eye with the back of her hand.

"I did everything I could to make them accept me, and I failed. I didn't fit the mold, but I couldn't live with their disapproval, because I loved them!" She was shouting now, tears streaming down her cheeks as she stared at her brother. "I loved them, Richard, and they hurt me again and again!"

Natalie felt a wave of sympathy for Helen. It sounded all too familiar. The Harriet that Natalie had known was mellowed by age, liberated by the death of her domineering husband. But it had come too late for Harriet to have a relationship with her daughter.

Natalie knew her own relationship with Harriet was a kind of surrogate mother-daughter bond, that Natalie was a replacement for Helen. The friendship only worked so well because Natalie and Harriet weren't related, didn't have a family history. Harriet had often spoken of her desire to reconcile with Helen, but neither of them had taken the first step, and now it was too late.

Helen slowly regained her composure. She sniffed and tossed her head defiantly. Ron looked at Helen as if he saw her for the first time. He opened his mouth to say something, then closed it.

Finally, Richard spoke. "You were too sensitive," he said, raising his gaze to Helen. "You were always too sensitive."

"A dirty word in our family, wasn't it, Richard?" Helen said. "You were raised to be tough, get on in the world, compete. Every Frazier had to make something of himself, prove he was worthy of the family name. It started way back with Old Frederick going off to Alaska to find gold, and Great-Grandpa, the lumber baron, who got rich selling redwood after the earthquake. Making money was the family religion, and when the Depression wiped them out, the Frazier men took it out on their families. And you proudly carry on the tradition of the family neurosis, waving it like some germ-infested banner from the Dark Ages."

"Don't talk to my husband that way!" Sheila yelled.

"He's my brother. I can talk to him any way I please."

"Look, Helen," Richard said with a tone of patience that surprised Natalie. "Let's forget the china and try to put aside our differences for the moment. We owe Harriet that much."

He paused for a second, as if gathering his thoughts. "We need to stick together. If the new will turns up, the family will contest it. It won't be hard to prove she was getting senile. The Bergstroms will back us up. Their daughter was here every day. It's important to do it legally."

"What about ethically?" Ron asked.

His father gave him a stern look, but didn't reply. Sheila rose and walked haltingly out of the house, slamming the screen door behind her. For a moment, no one spoke.

"As to your request, Miss Hughes," Richard said. "For my part, you're welcome to stay." He took out a new pack of cigarettes and slowly opened it. "It would be better to have someone in the house until things are settled. Please forgive us; we have these squabbles every time we get together. It's a family tradition."

Natalie wondered if his sudden kindness and invitation were meant to spite Helen. Or was he secretly hoping Natalie would find the will?

"Always the cool one, aren't you, Richard?" Helen said. "Always in control, just like Dad."

Richard looked at her a moment and something seemed to flash and disappear in his eyes, as if a memory had sparked and then dimmed.

"I'd love to fight with you, Helen, but I just don't have the energy anymore. Sorry." He grinned ruefully and shrugged.

Sheila came back in the house, lugging a box full of newspapers.

"I'm taking the china," she announced to no one in particular. "Harriet said I could have it." She stumbled over to the cabinet, opened the front, and began to clumsily remove the antiques and wrap them in newspaper. No one spoke.

"What about the tea cup that was supposed to be evidence?" Ron asked.

"They already checked it for prints," Richard said. "They didn't find any."

"You can have everything except the Limoges collection," Helen said. "That was Grandma's. It was supposed to be mine."

"She said I could have everything," Sheila said, placing a wrapped platter into the side of the box.

Helen walked over to the cabinet, reached inside, and removed a delicate china flower vase. "This vase is mine," she said triumphantly.

"You can't have it. Harriet gave it to me." Sheila grabbed Helen's arm, and Helen pushed her backwards.

"Harriet never liked you, anyway. Alcoholics remind her of Grandpa."

Sheila rocked back on her heels, put her face in her hands, and began to cry. Helen strode out of the room, vase in hand, and slammed the door.

Chapter Thirteen: The Trunk

Natalie spent the late afternoon counting shorebirds from her kayak. She paddled until she was exhausted, then drifted while she scanned the shoreline through pocket binoculars. Overhead an osprey shrieked, circling. It plunged feet first into the water, flapped its wings and flew away with a sun perch in its talons. Natalie wished she had brought something to eat so she could stay until sundown. But she, too, was a creature of routine. By seven o'clock her stomach ached.

Helen's car was the only one left in the driveway when Natalie returned to the house. Climbing the steps to her room, Natalie heard a muffled sob. At the end of the hallway the door to the attic stood open. The noise had come from above. Natalie climbed the ladder and peeked over the edge.

Helen lay curled on the floor in the far corner of the attic. She clutched something to her chest as swayed back and forth, sobbing miserably. A single, bare bulb cast a wan yellow light, barely illuminating an open trunk next to Helen.

"Are you all right?" Natalie asked.

Helen must not have heard. Eyes closed, she continued to cry. "I didn't mean it. I didn't mean it. I'm sorry."

As Natalie knelt beside her, Helen jumped, her eyes staring like a frightened child.

"Helen? Are you all right?"

Helen sat up and wiped her nose with a sleeve. She was holding a ragged teddy bear.

"I'm sorry. I just—I lost control for a moment. Do you happen to have a Kleenex?"

Natalie found a tissue in her pocket and handed it to Helen.

"I didn't mean to bother you," Natalie said. "I just heard a noise and thought—"

"I can see why she liked you," Helen said, loudly blowing her nose. "You're nothing like the rest of the family."

Natalie said nothing.

"She came to see me a month ago, and I was horrid," Helen said with a sigh.

"Harriet?"

"Yes. She said she was in the city on business and she decided to drop by. She should have called. Stephanie and I were in the middle of an argument when Harriet arrived without warning. Stephanie left. I knew Mother didn't like her, so I was angry to begin with."

Helen gently laid the teddy bear on the floor. Natalie pushed aside a bow and quiver of arrows and sat down.

"We had coffee together," Helen continued. "She was trying to tell me something, but she had a hard time getting it out. I think she wanted to apologize for what happened between us. I wasn't in the mood to listen. She always had a way of focusing on her own pain, ignoring me. Maybe she saw me as the stronger person." Helen laughed sadly and shrugged. "I don't think she ever really loved me."

Natalie put her hand on Helen's arm.

"You couldn't have known she would die."

"I came up here looking for the will, but as I was going through these old things I started looking for something that might tell me she cared. My old teddy was in the trunk, wrapped in tissue paper. She kept it." Helen picked up the bear and examined it. "The stuffing is almost all gone, and it's filthy, but she kept it." Helen dropped the teddy in her lap and covered her face as her shoulders shook.

Natalie sighed and patted Helen's back.

"Sometimes people aren't able to communicate with the ones most important to them," Natalie said. "Harriet knew she made a lot of mistakes as a mother, and I think that kept her from saying what she wanted. I think she loved you very much."

"I was so mad at her for dying before we had made peace. Even though it wasn't her fault. I'm not really such an awful bitch."

Natalie glanced away, and Helen laughed sadly.

"Steph says I get that way when I come back here. She says she can't stand to be around me when I'm with my family." She looked up at Natalie with the large eyes of a wounded child. "I was so jealous when I found you here and realized Mom had left you a note. She was always looking for a new daughter. Sheila was one." Helen blew her nose again. "I am glad you're here, Natalie. Really."

"Call me Nat."

"That's what Mother called you, isn't it?"

They sat for a few minutes in silence. There were footsteps below, and Ron's face popped up from the ladder.

"I saw your car still here, Helen. Is this a bad time?"

"No, come on up, Ron."

"I've already been through all this old stuff," Ron said. "The will's not up here, and you're not going to find anything interesting, because I already did." He waved a tattered, leather-bound notebook in his hand. "It's Carl Frazier's journal. He settled Schooner Bluff." Ron thumbed through the pages, stopped, began to read. "Here it is: 'February 25, 1860. On the night of the 16th, two Wiyot women and an elderly man came to my door. With them was a wounded child. Someone had attacked their village, Yachwanawach, and they sought help. The child had a most terrible gash on her head. I sent a hired hand for the doctor, who arrived some hours later but was unable to save the poor child.

"'The following day I heard news of a slaughter on an island in the bay. The names of the guilty were well known. I wished to speak against the killing, but the sentiment was against the Indians! An article had appeared in the paper calling for their destruction, and it must have incited some to act violently.

"'When I returned home, I sent the Wiyot family away. I wished no one to know I had sheltered them. May God have mercy on my coward's soul. Those poor savages had done nothing to deserve such treatment.'

"Later on he names the leader of the settlers who massacred the Indians. It was Rolf Bergstrom. He got away with it, too. Wouldn't the Clam Beach Register love to get a hold of this?"

"I dated Jack Bergstrom in High School," Helen said. "It took me a few years to figure out what a jerk he was. Now I understand why Mother wanted to sell the land back to the Wiyots. I'm in favor of it."

Helen suddenly looked like a different person to Natalie—strong, independent, her armor shed.

"Carol must have come looking for Rolf's diary," Natalie said. "I was at her house before the memorial and found a chapter of Harriet's memoirs there."

Ron raised one eyebrow.

"Harriet found a pot out in the ravine when she was little," Natalie said, "a pot at a gravesite. She thought there might have been some connection to the Anasazi, but who knows? What really matters is that it would establish a native presence here—something that would help the Wiyot claim that the property was their ancestral land."

"I can see why the Bergstroms wouldn't want to leave that lying around for us to find," Helen snorted. "But now their claim to grazing rights is in trouble. Ron, do you mind if I take Rolf's journal back to the hotel? I think it would be better to keep it in the safe there."

Ron nodded and handed the journal to Helen.

"Goodnight, you two," she said, and climbed back down the ladder to the hallway.

Ron and Natalie glanced at one another.

"Must be late," said Ron, running his hand through his hair and staring at the floor. "I guess I should head back to camp."

"You don't have to leave right away," Natalie said. "I'll be up for a while finishing my count—I wouldn't mind the company."

"Sure," Ron said with a grin, as Natalie climbed carefully down the ladder.

Ron settled down with a magazine and a glass of wine in an overstuffed chair in the living room, Waldo at his feet, while Natalie finished recording her daily count at a writing desk opposite him. It was quiet, the only sounds the ticking of a clock and the distant roar of breakers. Natalie was glad for the company. It felt good to have a man around, domestic.

The phone rang in the hallway, and Ron hopped out of the chair to answer it, Waldo staring after him. After a few moments, Ron came back into the living room looking worried. "I have to leave. Dad wants to talk to me. He's at his office in town. I'll drop Waldo by on my way back."

Natalie nodded. She sat and listened to Ron's footsteps leaving the house, the door closing, the car starting. The house felt empty without him. She went upstairs and turned on the tap in the bathtub, adding sandalwood oil. As she started to undress, the phone rang again. She turned off the tap and went downstairs to answer it. It was Henry Fishhawk.

"Miss Hughes, I was wondering if you could come over. I need your help."

"I'm kind of busy right now. Can it wait 'til morning?"

"No. That detective is here to arrest me. They found the murder weapon on my property."

Chapter Fourteen: The Arrest

Natalie followed Henry's directions to his mobile home. A county sheriff's car stood in front, headlights illuminating the home's metal walls. A deputy sat in the driver's seat with the door open, writing on a clipboard. Buck Davis's green Dodge blocked the carport.

As Natalie stepped out of her car, Henry appeared at the doorway to his home, hands behind his back, squinting in the glare from the headlights. He stepped out, and Natalie saw that he was handcuffed. Davis followed, still wearing his suit and tie from the funeral, with one hand on Henry's wrists. Davis looked strained, but Henry's expression was stoic.

"What's going on, Davis?" Natalie asked.

"We got a tip about the murder weapon. You were right. It was the adze. We found it in the bushes over there." He gestured with one hand. "And there was blood on the blade. We'll have it analyzed, but I'm sure it's Harriet Frazier's. Henry was at her house the day of the murder. It's enough to take him in."

"What about fingerprints?"

"We haven't been able to check them out, but we did find some on the adze."

"Who gave you the tip?"

"Someone called it in. A woman."

"Sounds to me like he's being framed."

“If so, he's safer in protective custody. Either way, I have to take him in.” Davis gave her a look that asked for understanding, but she stared at him coldly, fighting back anger.

For a moment she wondered if she could have been wrong. Maybe Harriet had been planning to back out of the land deal. Maybe Henry hadn't signed the will after all.

She looked into Henry's eyes, looked at Davis. Her intuition said Henry was innocent. It was enough.

“If Henry Fishhawk is a murderer, I'll kiss Phyllis Schlafley,” she said. She saw a twinkle in Davis's eyes, the beginning of a grin. His momentary lapse from officialdom gave her an opening.

“Look, Buck, this just doesn't feel right. If he killed her he wouldn't hide the weapon in such an obvious place. He's not stupid, and he had no motive. She was more valuable to him alive than dead. If we can't find the will, the family could pull out of the land sale.”

“It’s not a choice, Natalie. Please understand. You can have a few minutes to talk in private.”

Davis avoided her gaze as he walked past her to the car.

“What about Richard Frazier's car? Did you check that out?” she called to his back.

He turned around. “Richard Frazier was a hundred miles away. He has an ironclad alibi.”

“What about his wife?”

"She drives a blue Nissan, and she was driving it that day. Her husband had the Mercury. I checked with his secretary and the guy he met with. Mary Slocum didn't remember the right day, or she was lying."

"Why would she lie?"

"Ask him," Davis said, pointing to Henry. "Maybe she's trying to protect someone."

"Nat, I have a favor to ask you," Henry said.

"I'll get a good attorney, Henry, don't worry. This mess can be cleared up," Natalie said.

"I don't need a lawyer. I have one. She's the tribal attorney. I need you to take care of my dog."

Natalie looked around.

"She's inside," he said, gesturing with his head.

Natalie stepped inside. The mobile was small but immaculately clean, paneled in light-colored wood. The kitchen and living area were one room. It smelled of lemon-scented detergent. The sink was full of dishes, but the suds had gone.

A chrome and formica table with a typewriter stood next to the efficiency kitchen. There were several neatly arranged piles of papers and letters on the table, a piece of stationary with tribal letterhead stuck in the typewriter. Beneath the table were two cardboard filing boxes. A TV sat in a corner facing a short, striped couch. A pretty braided rug covered the floor. Bright chintz curtains hung in the windows.

A single fiery red geranium bloomed in a pottery planter on the windowsill. On one wall hung a leather ceremonial headband with flicker feathers attached to leather strings. A small pouch hung on the same peg. Through the bedroom door, Natalie caught a glimpse of uniform as one of the deputies searched through Henry's belongings. Natalie still didn't see a dog.

Henry stepped into the mobile and squeezed past Natalie. "Sophie's over here," he said, walking to a corner beside the couch.

Natalie followed him and saw something that looked like a streaked white mop curled up in a basket. Two black eyes and a nose peered out at Natalie. The dog rose stiffly, wagging its tail.

"She's pretty old," Henry said. "Fifteen, I think. The vet says she's going blind, but she has a real good sense of smell."

Natalie looked into the opaque eyes of the little dog and gave it a pat on the head. It opened its mouth, panting, showing rows of flat teeth.

"She plays with rocks. It's worn her teeth down. I could never break her," he said. "She can only eat soft dog food. I called my granddaughter, in LA. Ali can come up in a couple of days, then she'll take care of Sophie. She works in a research lab and someone has to take her place." There was sadness in his voice as he spoke. The reality of his situation seemed to be sinking in.

"I'll be glad to come over and take care of Sophie."

"I'd feel a lot better if you'd take her with you, Nat. She pines if I'm not here. The last time I was gone for a few days she stopped eating."

"But where would I keep her? I'm gone most of the day."

"She's happy as long as she gets to go for her walks in the morning and evening, you know. You could leave her in the kitchen with her basket. She won't wet in the house. Sophie's a good dog."

Natalie reached down and scratched Sophie behind one ear. "Of course I'll take her."

"I have two goats, but Mary Slocum can take care of them. Would you stop by her place and tell her what's happened? She's in the yellow trailer at the turn off. She's got some mean dogs—that's why I don't want to leave Sophie with her."

"This whole situation stinks, Henry."

He was silent for a moment, then nodded. "It does."

"Your fingerprints would have to be on the adze to prove anything."

"My fingerprints are all over it. I had it several weeks ago when I gave a talk at the high school. Mrs. Frazier let me take some stuff from the collection, and I lashed an obsidian blade to the stone handle to show how we used to cut slabs with it."

Natalie felt sick. She tried to think of something hopeful to say. "At least you have witnesses to the fact you handled it before the murder.

The whole thing about the adze and the phone tip will sound fishy to any jury. Aren't you angry?"

"I'm an old man. I don't have the energy to get mad. Better just to feel the sadness beneath the anger and get on with what I need to do." He nodded at the pouch hanging from the wall. "Would you take that, too, please? I might want you to bring it to me."

She took the pouch and stuffed it in the pocket of her jacket. Henry looked around the trailer, tears welling up in his eyes. He turned quickly and walked out the door.

The other deputy had disappeared into the bathroom. She heard him moving bottles around in the medicine cabinet. Natalie walked over to the wall above the table to look at a series of framed photographs.

One showed a much younger Henry and a woman who must have been his wife. She was pale, with a complexion more white than native. Next to that was a graduation picture of their daughter. A small gold sticker said Class of '70. Below that was a much older Henry in a more recent photo, with a little girl on a pony. Probably his granddaughter. She wondered where his daughter was.

Natalie thumbed through the books in Henry's bookcase. John Steinbeck, William Saroyan, Carlos Castanada, Loren Eisely. She pulled out a heavy handbook on California Indians by Kroeber, the anthropologist who had befriended Ishi. Maybe Henry would let her borrow it.

She searched the kitchen cupboards for dog food, found some, and placed it in a grocery bag along with the book. She carried the dog and the bag out to her van.

Henry was sitting in the back of the deputy's car. Natalie walked over and leaned down to the open window. "We'll have you out in no time. I promise," she said, reaching out and patting his shoulder. He managed a weak smile. "I found a book on California Indians. May I borrow it?"

He nodded. She felt tears forming in her eyes, bit her lip, turned and walked away.

Chapter Fifteen: Old Mary

Natalie rose late and took Sophie for a walk before breakfast. Buck Davis had admonished her to leave the night before, but she had promised only to think about it. Her words had conveyed more strength than she felt. In truth, she was ready to jump in the van and never come back.

And yet there was a part of her that didn't want to leave. Her greatest fear was to admit defeat, forced to live with failure. Each time she swayed toward the decision to leave, she imagined bulldozers tearing up the bottomland next to the bay. She imagined Henry growing old and sick in prison. She couldn't spend the rest of her life wondering what would have happened if she had stayed one more day.

Harriet must have mailed the will, the logical thing to do. She'd promised Natalie it would surface. Surely it was only a matter of time before Natalie found it. If nothing else, she had gained a sense of purpose from the whole thing, a purpose that outweighed the gnawing fear. Lying awake in bed the night before, she had toyed with the idea of buying a gun, thought about asking Ron to sleep at the house—for protection, of course—but she didn't know where he was. When she heard his truck in the driveway, she walked out to meet him with a feeling of relief.

Waldo hopped out of the pickup bed as Ron climbed out of the cab, looking exhausted. "Sorry I had to leave. What's up? You look terrible."

"That makes two of us," Natalie replied. "I haven't eaten breakfast yet, have you?"

"Just a cup of coffee. The most important part of a balanced breakfast, right?"

"Why don't I fix us an omelet?"

"That sounds great."

As Natalie whipped eggs and milk in the kitchen, she told Ron about the arrest. She poured the omelet into the pan and cut chives, added cheese.

"Where were you last night?" she asked, trying to sound unconcerned, and suddenly realized that she sounded like a jealous girlfriend. Her cheeks grew warm.

"At my parents' house. My dad and I had a long talk about my future. Well, he had a long talk, and I had a long listen. He's coming out here today with a friend, a developer. I plan to be somewhere else."

He was thumbing through the mail. He threw aside *Utne Reader* and *Quilter's Quarterly*, pulled out the local paper and sat reading while she cooked the eggs.

"Carol Bergstrom is at it again," he said, folding the paper into quarters and pointing to a small article as he handed it to Natalie. The headline read "Elderly Woman Murdered."

Natalie read aloud. "Mrs. Harriet Frazier of Schooner Bluff was found dead in her home on Wednesday. The police have determined the cause of death as homicide and are investigating the incident. The murder may be related to Mrs. Frazier's decision to change her will and deed most of her farmland to the Nature Conservancy. She was also selling sixty acres to a local Indian tribe.

"Suspects questioned include a wildlife biologist staying at Mrs. Frazier's bed and breakfast and a local tribal member who was seen at Mrs. Frazier's farm the day of the murder."

Natalie threw the paper down on the counter. "I'm going to pay Carol a visit after I see Mary Slocum. This is libelous! I've never been a suspect."

"But she was right about Henry," Ron said. "This was written before he was arrested. She's trying to get rid of you, but I doubt if she believes you had anything to do with Harriet's death."

Natalie dished up the omelet and sat down at the table. "That woman is... she's just... unscrupulous."

Ron grinned. "Thought you were going to say something else for a moment. You know, she's always been like this, but even though Harriet hated her they still managed to get along all right. This is the country—you have to make friendly with your neighbors."

"I wouldn't call murdering her 'getting along.'"

Ron raised one eyebrow. "So you think one of the Bergstroms killed Harriet?"

"Don't you?"

"They're at the top of my list. Who else lives close enough to break into the house and scare you like that the other day?"

"And it's quite possible Theresa guessed that Harriet was dying of cancer and told her parents," Natalie said, speaking excitedly as the connections fell into place in her mind. "She might have heard Harriet talking on the phone to the doctor's office, or noticed all the pain pills when she was cleaning. A murderer could justify killing an elderly person dying of cancer far more easily than if they were healthy."

Ron's face registered something that Natalie couldn't read, some memory or realization, but he didn't share it with her, and she didn't ask.

"I'm going to demand a retraction," Natalie said.

Ron rose and picked up his dish and utensils, started the dishwater.

She watched his back as she finished her meal, then added her dishes to his. "I have to visit Mary Slocum. Sophie is on the back porch. I'll see you later?"

He nodded, deep in thought, staring at his suds-covered hands.

When Natalie pulled up in front of Mary Slocum's yellow-striped mobile home, the old woman was sitting on the porch step smoking a cigarette. Some chickens and a pair of geese pecked at the bare ground in the yard. A fat little black dog ran to the car barking and wagging its tail. Mary's yard was as filthy as Henry's was immaculate, with broken lawn chairs scattered about and spindly plants struggling to survive in root-bound pots. A rusting truck that looked like it hadn't been driven in years was parked beside the trailer. Behind the house, a tethered goat chewed at the weedy grass beside a pile of empty rabbit hutches. An old flowerbed was dug up like a disturbed grave.

The old woman's face was wrinkled and dry, her hair in need of washing, but the bright blue eyes watching Natalie approach were alert and penetrating. Mary wore a green flannel shirt and a pair of jeans, with dirty pink scuffs completing the outfit. Her bare ankles resembled scaly turkey legs.

She gruffly called the dog back to her and waved her hand high in the air in greeting. As Natalie picked her way through boxes of aluminum cans and redemption bottles, the geese stretched their necks and honked a warning.

"Henry was arrested," Natalie said. "He told me you would take care of his goats if I asked you."

Mary took a long drag on her cigarette, blew the smoke out slowly, fixed her gaze on Natalie.

"When was he arrested?"

"Last night. They're charging him with murder."

"He didn't do it." She stubbed the cigarette out on the concrete steps.

"I know that, and you know that, but we have to prove it. I'm taking care of his dog, so you don't need to worry about her."

"Come on inside. I'll make some coffee."A smell like dirty dishrags wafted from the open door of the trailer.

Natalie shook her head. "I'd like to, but I only have a few minutes."

"Suit yourself."

"Did Mr. Davis ever take a statement from you about seeing Richard Frazier's car the day of the murder?"

"He wrote it down and said he might talk to me later."

"Do you remember what time you saw the car?"

"I know it was afternoon. I never start until after lunch. My favorite soap opera is on at eleven-thirty, and I never miss it. I walk for my health. People around here think I'm crazy because I wear loud clothes and a red baseball cap and sing to myself. But the singing helps me walk. Gives me energy. The clothes are so the cars will see me."

She took a pack of unfiltered cigarettes from the pocket of her shirt and carefully selected one. She lit the cigarette from a Bic lighter and took a long drag. Blowing the smoke out of her nose, she pointed to the road.

"My son was killed on that road. He was only eighteen. Been to a party and had too much to drink, so he decided to walk home. Hit and run. Whoever did it didn't even stop. That was thirty years ago."

She stopped and stared at the road as if seeing the incident in her mind for the millionth time. "Jack Bergstrom found him and took him to the hospital. But it was too late. He died the next day. Never regained consciousness. My husband left three months later. Couldn't deal with it."

Mary sat in silence for a moment, then added, "That was another unsolved murder, Miss..."

"Hughes."

"Miss Hughes. No one ever admitted to it. The police hardly investigated. They figured Charley was just a drunken half-breed—probably his own fault walking down the road late at night. Back then people thought that way about Indians. Some people still do."

"Maybe, but I don't believe most people think that way anymore. Still, if you grew up with it, I suppose it would make a person bitter," Natalie said.

"Charley and Jack were real close friends. Played football together. Bergstrom was the quarterback, Charley an end. Too bad Jack was the one who found him."

She shooed a chicken away with her foot.

"I don't think Jack ever got over it. He stops by to see how I'm doing now and then. Brings me a quarter of beef when they butcher. He gets my wood in for me in the fall. Brings a truck load and splits it right here. We talk about old times.

"I don't know why that Frazier woman wanted to deed her land away from the Bergstroms. They're fine people. Giving it to the birds, wasn't she?" She laughed and started coughing, a wrenching cough that shook her body.

"Did you take Harriet Frazier some willow bark the day she was murdered?" Natalie asked.

Mary narrowed her eyes. "I don't know anything about willow bark."

"It's used too treat chronic pain, isn't it? I believe you can boil it and make an infusion. Drink it as tea, a little bit at a time. It's easier on the system than tablets."

"Never used it myself. Wouldn't know." Mary stood up. "I'll take care of Henry's animals."

The old woman seemed very small and alone as she walked with Natalie to the van. Natalie had obviously hit a sore spot, but there was no way to know if Mary had actually been in the house the day of the murder. And if she was, why hide it? Mary stood watching as Natalie drove away. The fat black dog chased the van down the road to the turn off, then stood at the edge of the highway, watching.

Chapter Sixteen: The Valley Bulletin

No one was home at the Bergstroms', so Natalie drove into town to confront Carol at the newspaper office. Natalie mentally rehearsed what she'd say to Carol, growing more furious with each imagined scenario. By the time she pulled up in front of the newspaper office on Fern Valley's main street, her hands were shaking. She leaned her head on the steering wheel and breathed deeply, trying to regain her composure.

"The Valley Bulletin" arched in scrolled gold letters across the storefront window. Carol sat below, her face illuminated by a word processor on a huge wooden desk. Trophies lined a display case beside her. Citations, ribbons, pictures of Carol's daughter's basketball team, and framed news clippings covered the walls.

Harriet had once explained Carol as a lonely child, a cheater in school, the daughter of a heartless and demanding woman and, worst of all, very attractive.

A bell tinkled furiously as Natalie opened the door. Carol glanced up, her smile quickly fading.

Natalie slapped the newspaper down on the counter and said calmly, "This article is libelous, Mrs. Bergstrom. I have never been a suspect in Harriet's death. You can either print a retraction, or I'm going to sue you for every cent this paper is worth. I may sue you anyway."

"I'll do no such thing," Carol said, glaring at Natalie.

For a moment Natalie saw something like fear and desperation in the older woman's eyes. Then it was gone, replaced with coldness.

"This newspaper has an obligation to print the truth and to alert local citizens to anyone who can't be trusted."

"Does that include yourself, Carol? Breaking into Harriet's house to steal a chapter from her memoirs?"

"I don't know what you're talking about."

"You knew Harriet had something to use against you if you tried to block the land sale, and you went looking for it the night she was killed. But you found something else, something more interesting to someone like you—a chapter in her memoirs about a burial cave full of Indian artifacts. Too bad you missed the real leverage she had on you, Carol. Do you know what that is? A diary that proves your family was involved in a cover-up of the Wiyot massacre. How would you like to see that printed in the letters section of the Clam Beach Register?"

Carol's mouth dropped open, but she said nothing. Natalie glared at Carol, trying to hide a smirk.

"All right," Carol said. Her face relaxed. She suddenly looked very tired. "I'll print a retraction. But I was right about Fishhawk. I know he was arrested."

"He's being framed. A woman phoned in a tip."

"And you think I had something to do with it?"

"Let's just say I'm not ruling it out."

The bell behind Natalie jingled, and an elderly woman stepped through the door. Carol hurriedly composed herself. Natalie gave one last, savage glare, then stalked outside.

The next stop was the local Western Auto to buy spark plugs. A man in overalls chatting with the clerk fell silent and stared at her. She recognized him from the memorial service. In the grocery store, two women bent their heads together and whispered when Natalie stopped to select a head of lettuce. People were watching her. Even if Carol printed a retraction, the damage was done. Natalie hurriedly bought a few groceries and left.

Back at the Blue Heron, Natalie called every local charity and museum she could think of on the chance that Harriet had mailed a package to one of them. No luck.

She spent the rest of the morning on the bay, spotting birds. Five brown pelicans were fishing from the piling of an old pier. An immature bird with dark head and white underparts stayed on the piling when the others flew off. Using her binoculars, Natalie spotted an indentation around its neck, maybe a fishing line. She would call her boss to get help bringing it in. Two people were needed to subdue such a large bird.

The sun shone brightly. It was hot in the kayak. Fifty yards away a family tumbled out of a van. The father carried a chubby baby in a carrier. The mother, wearing a sun hat and bikini, passed out shovels and buckets to two older children. A shaggy dog ran back and forth along the waterline, scattering sanderlings.

The familiar longing, never forgotten for long, drew taut lines around Natalie's throat and chest. This was what she had planned when she and Mark had first married, but he was always too busy with research to raise a child. An associate professorship at San Jose State, long trips to South America studying the earliest New World settlements, and through it all the promise of "one more year."

Then he published a paper that became nationally famous. The next summer a major university offered him a full professorship in the Midwest. Natalie, mapping riparian habitat on the Sacramento River, was to join him in the fall. Two weeks before her assignment was finished, he phoned and told her about the other woman. The divorce papers were already in the mail.

Now she didn't even have a home, nothing but a few boxes and pieces of furniture in a storage locker. Even her two-timing cat had left her for a neighbor, lured away by sirloin tip. Not so different from her husband after all.

"There's no point in wallowing, Nat. Pull yourself together. You've got a job to do," she said aloud. She wiped her eyes and paddled back to shore.

At noon she took a sandwich and thermos from her pack and climbed the nearby bluff to a cool spot beneath a leaning cypress. She closed her eyes, leaned back against the rough trunk, and dozed.

The sound of an engine in the pasture below brought her to her feet. She didn't recognize the white pickup. She took out her pocket binoculars and scanned the truck's painted logo: Harper Construction.

Richard Frazier stepped out of the passenger side, a tall, gray-haired man from the other. They walked across the pasture pointing and gesturing, not at plants or animal sign, but at imagined curbs and future homes.

She put the binoculars back in her shirt pocket, sat down, rested her forehead on her knees. Tears stung her eyes, and she realized that like Richard and his business partner, she too had seen something more in the pasture below: a treehouse of scavenged boards precariously arranged in an old oak, a creek running below, her sister Maggie hanging from a branch above.

Possum Creek. That's what they had called it when they were little, before Maggie was lost to telephone calls, hair styles, painted nails. Before the old oak was cut and the creek filled in by developers building a new mall.

Natalie had stayed in her room for two days, crying or staring at the wall. She told her family she was sick. No one came in to talk to her. The energizing solitude of Possum Creek seemed stifling at home, with the others moving around just outside her door, so far away.

Suffering alone when something bad happened seemed normal to Natalie. When she emerged from her room she was numb, no longer a child, because she had lost the only safe place to be a child. Not long after that, her father was transferred again and the family moved to another state.

Natalie looked up and wiped her eyes. A cypress leaf drifted down like a lost feather. The grasses of the pasture bent, shimmering, in the wind, like the beating wings of a vast bird.

Gazing at the slough and the bay beyond, Natalie realized she had once again found a safe sanctuary, had become an intricate part of a place, had opened herself to love. She stood up. This time would be different. This time she would fight. She was an adult. She had weapons. Harriet's will was a weapon. The law requiring a permit and impact report from developers was a weapon. A rare species of owl's clover grew in a salt marsh along the spit, and the regular biologist knew where to find Point Reye's bird's beak. The very same endangered plants threatened by the development provided legal tools to fight back.

Natalie smiled. She wasn't afraid, and she wouldn't give up. Her usual fears and doubts were gone. Suddenly she was in the mood for a good fight.

She walked down the path to the slough, feeling for the first time in a long while a heady glow of confidence. Richard Frazier and his friend stood at the bottom of the path, waiting.

Chapter Seventeen: Development

Richard Frazier and the other man fell briefly silent at the look on Natalie's face.

Richard spoke first. "This is Miss Hughes, Harry. She's a wildlife biologist. Works on the bay."

A big man with a bulging stomach, Harry narrowed his eyes as Richard introduced him to Natalie.

"Harry Metcalf," Richard said. "Harry is on the County Board of Supervisors."

Natalie stood with her hands on her hips. She gave Metcalf a perfunctory nod. He stared at her without blinking, obviously sensing an adversary.

"I hope you plan to file an Environmental Impact Report before you bring in the bulldozers," she said. Her voice was strained. Her heart pounded in her chest, and her face was hot.

"We'll go through the necessary channels," Richard said. He seemed sure of himself, his eyes mocking and superior, as if he found Natalie amusing. No wonder Helen hated him. "Any luck finding the phantom will?"

"No."

"Even if you do, it will be contested. Really, Miss Hughes, this isn't the right battle. This development will be carefully designed to protect the environment. It will be a model for others to follow. I really think you'll be happy when you see the results."

"I think I'll be happy when I find where Harriet hid the will. And I'm already happy now that I have an idea where it is."

Richard's expression changed abruptly, became menacing, and one arm stiffened as though he might hit her. He regained control just as quickly. "Maybe we'll contest the will on the grounds that you manipulated her. Maybe it was you who actually killed her."

Natalie glared at him, her fists clenched. She was afraid to open her mouth because all her thoughts were profane. When she didn't answer, Harry grinned, Richard nodded in satisfaction, and they turned and walked away.

She stood for a few minutes, trying to regain control. Why had she told him she knew where the will was hidden when she really had no idea? Simply to bait him, see his reaction? No. It was because somehow she knew Harriet had hidden it in such a way that Natalie would eventually stumble across it. Even now, when she thought about it, the solution to the riddle seemed just out of reach, waiting for the right combination to click into place. She sensed that she was near, even if she couldn't logically explain why.

Finally she put the kayak away, gathered her gear and walked back up the bluff. At the top, she watched as the two men got back into the truck and drove away. She saluted them with her middle finger.

At home she brought Sophie outside for company while she changed the spark plugs in the van. It took concentration, and she hoped that focusing on something would cool her down. After twenty minutes of trying to get the plug out of the number three cylinder head, she sat down on the grass, frustrated and angry. Her hay fever was bothering her, and she rubbed absentmindedly at her itchy eyes with grease-covered fingers. Sophie glanced up at Natalie's emphatic cursing, then settled back down onto the gravel.

A crunch on the driveway behind her made her jump. Waldo raced up to sniff Sophie and had his nose snapped for his efforts. He backed off, looking hurt, and lay down a few feet away.

Ron strode quickly across the lawn, hands in his pockets.

"Sounds like you're rehearsing a George Carlin routine," he said. "It's nice to know you don't always speak in perfect, polite sentences."

"I can't get the plug out of the number three cylinder," she said, feeling her cheeks flush.

"Well, I'm not surprised. It looks like you were using your face instead of your hands."

He wiped at her cheek and held up his grease-covered thumb with a smile.

Natalie shrugged. "I've been trying to infiltrate the local band of raccoons, see if they know anything about the will."

"Good one," Ron said appreciatively.

He picked up the plug wrench and had the plug out in a few seconds. She realized how much she missed having a man in her life. Someone who could handle the extra torque.

"Want me to put the new one in?"

"Sure. I'm not proud."

"Are you all right?" he asked, tightening the new plug into place.

"I told Carol Bergstrom about the diary you found."

"That should shake her up. But the damage to you is already done. This is tight little community. The whole idea is to run you out of town."

He straightened up and wiped his hands on a rag hanging over the bumper, then turned to watch as a green pickup drove into the driveway. Natalie's boss, Earl Cummings, parked in the open space and climbed slowly out of the pickup. He paused for a moment, fiddled with his glasses, smoothed back what few strands of white hair he had left, then walked over to them.

"Hello, Natalie. I was hoping to find you here." His tone lacked its normal joviality.

"I bet you've heard about the new housing development," she said. "I already talked to Frazier and the construction engineer about an E.I.R."

"Natalie, I need to... ah... I should ask you to take a leave of absence."

Ron's eyebrows shot up in surprise.

"I only have another month to go," Natalie said. "Are you saying I'm fired?"

"No, no, not at all. I'm just asking you to take a leave of absence until this... thing is all cleared up, and your name is off the list of suspects."

Her voice rose. "My name was never on the list of suspects. You can ask Sergeant Davis."

Earl wiped the palms of his hands on his pants. "This is a small community," he said quietly. "We have an image to uphold at Fish and Wildlife."

Ron snorted, and Earl glanced at him in surprise.

"So you're letting me go because a small town newspaper editor has a vendetta against me?" Natalie asked.

Earl fumbled at his pockets and took out a piece of paper, stared hard at it. "We're, uh, we're dealing with some other people here."

"You mean your boss?"

"Yeah."

Natalie looked at him in silence. He shifted uneasily on his feet.

"I'm really sorry, Natalie."

"Who's taking my place?"

"We have someone coming in temporarily. I need your records."

"You don't even want me to break in the new person?"

"I can do it."

"I've got a sick pelican that needs to be brought in. I'm going to need help doing it."

"Yeah, uh, I might be able to get someone out here tomorrow."

“Did my father have anything to do with this?” Ron asked.

Earl glanced back at his truck, as if considering his escape routes. “I think it was the County Board of Supervisors. They don't like to see ag land become a wildlife preserve.”

“Jesus, Earl!”

Earl cringed as if he’d been slapped.

“Richard Frazier wants to turn it into a housing development,” Natalie said. “Surely Fish and Wildlife is opposed to that? Or are you in the real estate business now?”

Earl put up his hands, palms out. “We just need to take this slowly, okay? Nice and slow. One thing at a time.”

“There isn’t any time! This land has to be protected, now.”

“Well, yeah, Fish and Wildlife wants to add land to the refuge, but cattle grazing brings in money. Coastal Commission doesn’t like converting agricultural land, either. If the Nature Conservancy gets it...” Earl shrugged.

“And Richard Frazier has offered to sell some of the land to Fish and Wildlife?” Natalie said.

Earl swallowed. “I don't suppose you were the one who convinced her to deed it to the Conservancy?”

“The will hasn't even been found.”

“You're in this really deep, Nat. It sure doesn't make us look very good.”

"It depends on who's doing the looking, Earl." She turned on her heel and walked inside. Her notes were on the writing desk in the living room alongside her notebook. She fought back tears as she gathered them, not bothering to put anything in order.

When she came out, Earl was sitting in his truck with the motor running. Natalie shoved the material at him.

"Here's what you want."

His face registered no emotion as he backed up and drove away.

Ron looked at her sympathetically. "I have to go to town for supplies, but how about getting together tonight? I make a pretty good lasagna. It's the only thing I know how to cook, so I've had a lot of practice." He reached over and squeezed her shoulder.

Natalie laughed, then choked back a sob. "Thanks," she said. "I could use some cheering up."

"You'll be all right?"

She nodded, and watched as he walked away. It felt good to have at least one friend. Hugging herself, she went into the house. She needed to find something to keep her busy.

Natalie picked up the phone book, looked up the number for the California Coastal Commission. The woman she talked to said the permit hadn't been filed. She sounded concerned when Natalie described the proposed development.

Next she called Buck Davis. Natalie told him about the hit and run death of Charley Slocum and asked him to check the files. She wanted to talk to Mary Slocum again. The woman was withholding something. The fact that Jack Bergstrom had found Charley, then taken care of the boy's mother for twenty years after Charley's death, made Natalie wonder. Twenty years was a long time to chop someone's wood. Unless you'd killed their son.

Chapter Eighteen: Romance

Ron was an excellent cook. As Natalie buttered a loaf of French bread, he opened a bottle of Chianti, poured a glass for each of them, then added an ample amount to the sauce. He made his own salad dressing with olive oil and wine vinegar with tarragon and tossed it over a mix of greens.

They sat in the living room chairs afterward, sipping glasses of wine. Waldo lay on the braided rug in front of the fireplace. Sophie, curled into a fuzzy ball, snored on the sofa.

"So tell me about yourself, Nat," Ron said, leaning forward. "Tell me your secret loves and desires."

Natalie wondered how much wine he had drunk. The bottle was three quarters empty, and she was only starting her second glass.

"Well, there's not much to tell. I became a biologist because I love plants and animals, being outdoors. I'm an environmentalist because I think it's all being destroyed. Pretty simple."

"Are the environmentalists winning?"

"No, but you I don't think you want to hear a dissertation on the state of the environment."

"Don't you think you'll burn out eventually?"

Natalie sighed. "I suppose so. Someday I want to settle down and live in a nice house in the country, raise a family. I imagine myself going to potlucks, carrying a baby around in a pack, growing masses of tomatoes and marigolds, canning pickles. Sound weird?"

"I thought you were a city girl."

"I grew up in the Midwest. My grandparents were farmers. I've never felt completely at home in the city. Being here the past few weeks just feels... right." She suddenly felt a little embarrassed at revealing so much. "You know, I called the Coastal Commission earlier."

Ron put his glass down. "What did they say?"

"They can't do anything until a permit is filed. They put me on a mailing list, so when it comes up I can check on it."

"Want to know a secret? I think Dad is planning to get around the wetlands thing by trading a marsh up north near a bird sanctuary. Audubon has had their eye on it for years."

"That happens a lot. Trading useless land to drain water from more profitable areas."

"He's been planning this for years. Courting friends in high places, planting favors to call in later."

"How do you know all this?"

"He told Helen about it last Christmas. He's always wanted to be filthy rich, and filthy is exactly the right word for it."

"If I find that will, he can forget about that. How would you testify if it went to court? You were here this summer. You know Harriet wasn't senile."

"No, she wasn't, but I hope it doesn't come to that."

"I called all the local charities and churches to see if they had received a package from Harriet. No luck. And I contacted both museums in the area. Ron, I'm beginning to doubt it will turn up."

He had beautiful eyes that looked straight at her. Didn't he ever blink? It was hard to hold his gaze for more than a few seconds.

"I admire your courage. Ignoring threats, questioning neighbors, going undercover in raccoon bands," he said.

"It's a pretense." She laughed, leaned over and stroked Sophie, who stretched her legs. "I'm not really brave at all. For most of my life I've felt as if some weird force was pulling me along while I screamed and kicked and tried to go the other way, toward security. I often do what I do out of fear."

He looked puzzled.

"Fear of what will happen if I don't act. Fear of fear. Does that make any sense?"

"Well, at least you're not afraid to be honest. I like that," he said. He raised his glass to her in a toast.

Blue jays began squawking outside. Ron turned toward the windows. Natalie jumped up and ran past him, out the French doors to the porch.

Harriet's yellow tabby crouched in the garden, watching something in the bushes. Probably a fledgling.

"Scat!" Natalie yelled. "Get out of here!"

The cat turned to look at her, waiting to see if she was really going to do something. She picked up a seashell from a collection on the banister and lobbed it at the cat. He darted for the pasture, then stopped the moment he was safely out of reach and began licking his back.

Ron came to the doorway and leaned against the wall. They stood side by side for a moment, looking out at the clouds growing pink in the sunset. Natalie could hear the breakers of the incoming tide hitting the rocks. A soft breeze blew in the house from outside.

"Come to the window, sweet is the night air," Ron said quietly.

She looked at him suddenly.

"Matthew Arnold," she said. "Dover Beach."

"Corny, right?"

She shook her head. He continued reciting as he stared out into the twilight.

"Ah, love, let us be true
To one another! For the world which seems
To lie before us like a land of dreams,
So various, so beautiful, so new,
Hath really neither joy, nor love, nor light
Nor certitude, nor peace, nor help for pain;
And we are here as on a darkling plain.
Swept with confused alarms of struggle and flight.
Where ignorant armies clash by night."

He turned to look at her, his face full of pain and longing.

"You have the most amazing eyes," he said.

Then he stepped forward, took her chin gently in his hand, and kissed her sweetly on the mouth, lingering for what seemed a long while. She put her arms around his neck, looked into his eyes, and returned the kiss. She could smell the fresh scent of his hair cream.

The phone rang.

"It's only a phone," he said.

She wanted him, but she stepped away. "I'll just be a minute," she said. "It might be Buck with some information for me."

She walked into the hallway feeling dizzy, from the wine, or the kiss, or both. She picked up the phone and paused before answering.

"Hello," she said breathlessly.

"Miss Hughes?" It was a woman's voice.

"Yes."

"This is Allison Baker, Henry Fishhawk's daughter."

"Oh, yes."

"I need to get in touch with Ron Frazier. Do you think you could give him a message?"

"He's here right now. I'll put him on."

She walked back to the living room, feeling suspicious. She told Ron it was for him, but didn't give him a name. He shot her a quizzical look and walked into the hallway.

Natalie sat by the hallway entrance and listened. The woman was obviously more than a mere acquaintance. His tone told her everything. She felt her cheeks grow hot and poured another glass of wine. When he came back into the living room she avoided his gaze.

"I didn't realize the Allison you mentioned was Henry's daughter," she said. Her tone was as neutral as she could manage.

"It was over between us eight months ago. It's still over."

"But she'll be here in the next few days."

"And I plan to avoid her."

He sat down next to her and reached out to put an arm around her. She stood up. "I'm exhausted. It's been a hard day. Thanks for cooking dinner and helping clean up."

She sensed his disappointment, but jealousy and anger were all she could feel. He smiled weakly, said good night and walked out the door. The moment he left, she realized she had made a mistake.

He had left a cotton sweater on the sofa, an easy excuse for her to follow, or for him to come back. She put it around her shoulders, walked out the door, and sat on the porch swing. She swayed back and forth, her mind blank, watching the twilight fade, listening to a tree frog croaking in the distance. The sweater had a sweet, musky smell. She touched her lips and could still feel the kiss, see the longing in his eyes. Finally she rose, walked down the steps and across the yard.

A bright, full moon floated in the east, lighting the path through the pasture. She pulled the sweater tightly around her shoulders against the cool air flowing down the hill. An owl winged silently overhead, searching for field mice. As its shadow swept across the silvered grass, something scurried across the path and disappeared into the bushes.

She made her way down into the ravine. The blue dome of the tent was lit from the inside, casting Ron's silhouette on the wall. He knelt on the tent floor, studying something in his heads. She tiptoed around to the entrance and peered in at his back, trying to think of something witty to say. Then she saw the Anasazi pot in his hands.

Chapter Nineteen: Depression

Waldo, lying on the floor of the tent, opened his eyes and thumped his tail. Natlie turned and crept away. Glancing back, she saw Ron stand in the tent. Had he heard her? As soon as she reached the path she ran. She threw the sweater down inside the door of the house and sat on the sofa, breathless, shocked, angry.

When did he take the pot? Was he worried someone might steal it? But surely he would have told her. As an heir to the estate, was he actually stealing? She was sure of only one thing. He had lied to her, and she couldn't trust him. One more person in her life had let her down. Sophie woke up and sniffed Natalie's arm, then licked the teardrops from her cheek.

Natalie sat in the darkness as the moon rose, a square of pale light marching slowly across the rug. She didn't move. It was something she had learned as a child—sit still without moving until the pain goes away and the numbness takes over, until you don't feel anything. It was a childish way of coping with disappointment, but it was all she had. Hours later, she awoke, stumbled upstairs with Sophie, and fell into bed.

The next morning, Natalie sat at the breakfast table picking at a grapefruit and sipping coffee. She stared out the window at heavy gray clouds overhead. A darkness settled over her, an internal veil that clouded her thoughts. She was stupid to have thought that she could stop anything, could fix anything. She could no more solve

Harriet's death than she could solve her own failed marriage, could no more prevent the destruction of the pasture than stop the destruction of a ramshackle treehouse.

She sat, unmoving, imagining conversations. First with her boss, then with Richard Frazier. It always happened this way, mental dialogues repeated over and over, paralyzing her.

She saw Harriet's lifeless body, felt the weight of her friend's death, and then the weight fell away as a sense of fury exploded within Natalie. She hated Harriet for leaving her here, slipping off into the shadow land of death to escape the problems of the world. She hated Buck Davis for arresting Henry and Henry for submitting without a fight. She shook with impotent rage. She would never find the will. The land would be lost to Richard Frazier's yuppie condos. The real murderer would go free. Henry's people would never come home. Her stomach clenched, and for a moment she was afraid that she would vomit.

Something thudded against the window. A hummingbird. It fell, grabbed onto a branch of fuschia outside, righted itself, and sat stunned. She watched it for a moment, waiting for it to collapse and fall from the branch. Then it darted away.

She breathed out a long, shuddering sigh and rose. Ron's pickup puttered along the driveway. Natalie peered out the window and saw Waldo hanging out the window as the truck drove past.

Her vision narrowed, darkened, and the anger was back in an instant. The one person she thought she could trust was as stupid and weak as the rest of them. He'd only managed to hide it better. And she'd been blinded by his charm. Maybe he was the killer. Maybe he had done it to steal from Harriet's collection, from Harriet's land. What did it matter? Natalie couldn't do anything about it, just like always.

She thought of the time after the divorce when she had spent whole days in bed, only rising to eat a meal or go to the bathroom. Other days she could barely pick herself up to go to work. Some weekends she spent sitting and brooding for hours, inactive and bitter. Crying helped relieve the pain, but mostly she felt numb. Nothing touched her, nothing mattered. She moved through life as if walking through a heavy liquid, one slow step at a time, everything vague and distorted.

Natalie clutched the back of the chair. Remembering how terrible it had been before frightened her, but she was sinking into it again, falling...

Harriet would have known what to say to cheer Natalie up, to shake her out of it. Probably something totally inappropriate, delivered with a naughty twinkle in her eye. Natalie choked and began to sob, an overwhelming sorrow washing away the blank anger and despair.

Outside the tall windows, hummingbirds buzzed around the pink and purple trumpet flowers of the fuschia. A male Anna's hummingbird, green with a scarlet crown, hovered next to the window for a moment to look in at Natalie, then buzzed away. Next a brown Rufous appeared, and the Anna's came back and tried to drive it away. She could hear their tiny, shrill wingbeats as they attacked and retreated, never touching, even as they flew suicidally close. They moved away to hover in mid-air then darted in for the attack, zinging back and forth twice, three times, until Rufous left and Scarlet Crown won the day, but only for a moment. Then he too left.

Natalie wiped her cheeks. In the past she often lifted herself up from the edge of depression by doing something very ordinary, grounding. An African violet on the windowsill looked dry. There were plants throughout the house which probably hadn't been watered for days. She found a pitcher in the cupboard, filled it with water, added a few drops of plant food.

Sophie scratched at the back door and whined to be let in. The little dog lay down by her dog food bowl, but ignored the food in it. Natalie put down the pitcher and focused on the dog. Natalie tried bacon, milk, cheese. The dog looked away. Sophie was pining for Henry—she hadn't eaten since yesterday's breakfast, and then she had only nibbled at part of an omelette. Henry would know what to do until his granddaughter arrived.

Natalie watered the kitchen and dining room plants, threw out dried roses from a vase. She searched for other plants that had been neglected. Harriet's taste wasn't exotic. Swedish ivy and philodendron could survive without frequent watering. A Christmas cactus in the upstairs master bedroom had begun a summer bloom. Natalie opened the cream-colored curtains in the fronting bay window, which had been drawn to let the last guests sleep in, and saw the sun breaking through the clouds. The bright rays pierced the gloom, lifted her spirits.

She turned to leave the room, then stopped suddenly, her hand on the doorknob. Looking back, she felt that something was missing. She quickly scanned the room. She and Ron had searched the upstairs rooms thoroughly, but something still bothered her. A thought tickled the back of her mind. She tried to call it up, but it fluttered just out of reach. The lamps were in place, and all the furniture and paintings seemed to be there. A lacy afghan covered the bed. The phone rang. She closed the door, still feeling a nagging suspicion, and descended the stairs.

Chapter Twenty: Roses

When Natalie picked up the phone, Buck Davis was on the line.

"I checked the record on the Slocum case," he said. "Jack Bergstrom was the driver."

Natalie caught her breath. "Did anyone see?"

"There was one witness—Helen Frazier was in the car with Bergstrom. Slocum was walking down the road and stepped out to thumb a ride, but Jack and Helen were arguing and didn't see Slocum until it was too late. The Bergstroms and Fraziers managed between them to hush up the whole thing. The sheriff wrote in the record that it was probably Slocum's fault and not a matter of negligence. The file was marked confidential. I don't want you to let this out before I question Mary Slocum again. Got it?"

"I'll keep it to myself." She told him about the discovery of the Anasazi pot in Ron's tent, but left out how she had come to be there.

"Why do you think he took it?" Davis asked.

"I think he was afraid someone else might get to it first. It's the key to his whole theory, the link to anything he discovers at the dig. But I don't know why he didn't tell me he had it. Maybe he was worried I'd tell someone."

She filled him in on other recent events: the loss of her job, Carol Bergstrom's article, Richard Frazier's plans for the farm.

"What if Fishhawk isn't the killer, Nat? I can't guarantee you protection." His voice was stern.

"I won't go if there's still a chance of finding the will. I can't say why, but I'm halfway hopeful for the first time in days. I'm driving in to Clam Beach to see Henry this morning. Are you going to be around?"

"I have to be in court all day, tomorrow too. Give me a call if anything turns up."

The jail was at the end of a long corridor in the courthouse, behind a thick wood door. An orange vinyl sofa with stuffing peeking out from several tears dominated the tiny waiting room. A long-haired man leaned forward on the sofa, arguing quietly and gesturing frantically to a young man in suit and tie standing beside him.

Natalie gave her name at the window, then stood and waited until a female guard escorted her into an even smaller, windowless room with a pair of folding chairs on either side of a card table. Natalie sat down on one of the chairs, put her chin in her hands, and stared at a peace symbol drawn in black marker on the table.

She waited several minutes before Henry appeared. He seemed to have aged years since she had last seen him, but brightened when he recognized her. Natalie took his hand and held it a few minutes.

"I came to see if you needed anything and to tell you Sophie is all right, but she's stopped eating."

He sat down heavily in the opposite chair. "When all else fails, the thing she loves most is pasta. Plain old Ragu sauce and spaghetti." He peered quizzically at her. "You could have just called me on the phone to ask me that."

"I wanted to see how you were doing."

Henry shrugged helplessly and spread his hands. "I'm okay. Friends come to see me night and day, bring pies and cookies. Everyone seems worried about my health in here. The tribal leaders were going to mortgage a bunch of property to pay for the bond, but I wouldn't let 'em."

"I think you should. You're not going to skip bail."

"I might. My fingerprints match the ones on the adze, Natalie. If it looked like I was going to jail for good, I don't think I'd stick around."

"They don't have anything else on you. You'll get off."

Henry raised one eyebrow. "You seem pretty certain of that. Even if I do get off, what happens if the real killer isn't found? Jack Bergstrom is already collecting signatures of landowners on the Bluff who oppose the land sale. Did you visit Mary Slocum?"

"Yesterday."

"What did you think of her place?"

It seemed like an odd question to Natalie. "I don't know what you mean."

"It's a junkyard, isn't it?"

Natalie could feel her cheeks growing red with embarrassment. "It wasn't that bad. A little cleaning up..."

"See? A lot of the ranchers are opposed to the sale 'cause they think we're going to move in a bunch of mobiles and landscape with abandoned cars. You know, they might be right." He leaned back in his chair and stared at Natalie with the same intensity as when they first met.

She stared down at the table and traced the outline of the peace symbol. "I don't see how that's relevant."

"It's damn relevant! What do you think of this jail?"

She tried to imagine what he wanted her to say, searched for the right answer, came up with nothing.

"No opinion?" he said. "Well, I think it's a big piece of junk. This whole town is a big piece of junk. Concrete, signs, cars. You can't even see the bay until you practically fall into it. But because it's white man's junk, and you paint it and replace the old stuff with the new, it's called progress."

Natalie thought she was beginning to understand where he was going.

"Mary's place is typically Indian—stereotypically Indian. She doesn't care about appearances. Mine isn't. But Mary is more true to her heritage than I am, because she refuses to see things like white people. She's not possessed by her possessions. Of course, she's never going to make any soap commercials." He smiled to himself, then reached out and tapped the table with his forefinger. "The reason I wanted to buy Harriet's land is because it was our land once, and we belong there. Not everyone in the tribe knows it, but the place misses us. It's calling us back. You may not believe it, but that's the truth."

"I believe you, Henry."

"But the people who stole it, those clean white Scandinavians, they think it would be horrid to have the beauty of the place spoiled by an Indian rancheria. They let their cows shit all over our burial places, but they worry about a few abandoned cars."

Natalie nodded, beginning to feel as though she were being lectured. "Okay. I see your point."

"I don't want the tribe to blow my arrest up into a racial issue. Nothing could be worse for my people. We need to start healing past wounds, not making new ones. And the whites will use it as an excuse to block the land sale. If I go to trial it's going to polarize the community and send us all back to the bad old days. Now are you beginning to see?"

She let out a long breath. "Yes."

"So you have to find the real killer."

She sat up abruptly and leaned forward. "You want me to take out an ad in the personals?"

"Don't be ridiculous."

"I don't even know where to begin."

Henry shrugged. "Use your intuition," he said, as if nothing could be simpler. "Harriet said it's pretty good."

"Well, I don't know about that," she said, thinking of her husband. "But at least Buck Davis is an honest detective, and I'm sure he'll realize his mistake once he looks at the facts."

"He likes you. I can tell. You could use it to help me."

"Now you're being sexist."

Henry laughed bitterly. "Well, I'm a desperate old Indian who doesn't want to live out his life in jail. It's not a coincidence you came when you did. There's no such thing as coincidence. It was meant to be."

"And I'm supposed to believe that? Aren't you just appealing to some white woman's fascination with mysticism, or at least her racial guilt?" The moment she said it, she felt sorry.

Henry's face fell. "It doesn't matter one bit if you believe it or not. It's true." He turned away to cough into his hand. When he turned back he looked drained. "Stealing our land wasn't the worst thing the whites did to my people, Natalie. The worst thing they did was take our honor. Don't let them keep us from getting it back."

She reached over and squeezed his hand. "Henry. I give you my word I'll do everything I possibly can to help. But I'm only one person, and I have limited resources."

"You have more resources than you're aware of, Natalie."

He stood abruptly, said goodbye, and knocked on the door for the guard to open it. As she watched him shuffle down the hallway toward his cell, Natalie was gripped with a sense of grief and foreboding. She felt he had asked too much of her. She was up against a very cunning murderer, and the police were not on her side. Finding the will had been uppermost in her mind, but now it seemed secondary to proving Henry's innocence. The racial overtones of the matter only made it worse.

She was torn between shame for what had happened to Henry's people and anger that she should feel that way. Why should she suffer for something the whites did a hundred years ago? Maybe it wasn't necessary to feel guilty about the past. Maybe all that was called for was to take some responsibility for the future. That's what Harriet had tried to do.

Back at home, Natalie watched Sophie lick clean a bowl of spaghetti. A pile of Harriet's mail lay on the counter, and Natalie thumbed through it absentmindedly. A letter from the County Fair Committee had already been opened, probably by Ron. Natalie glanced at a receipt for Harriet's entry of several roses in the fair. She remembered Harriet's last letter: "Don't let Carol Bergstrom steal my roses for the fair."

Was it really that important to Harriet, or was the message a clue? What if Harriet had mailed the package to the fair? Natalie's heart pounded. Of course! Harriet knew Natalie loved county fairs. They had planned to go together. But what kind of display item would hide a piece of paper, and why wasn't there a receipt for it? The entry blank said that the flower entries were due today between 9:00 A.M. and

7:00 P.M. They were categorized by color and type. That gave her an idea.

Natalie found a cardboard box, two large empty coffee cans on the back porch, and pruning shears in the garden shed. On the south side of the bungalow, Harriet's roses were in full bloom. The weeds had grown tall, but she had kept the roses watered and pruned. Natalie felt a pang in her stomach and wished Harriet had confided in her about the illness. Why had she tried to face it alone? I was raised never to be a burden to anyone. The remembered words brought tears to Natalie's eyes. Had Harriet really chosen to face her illness alone? Who else had known? At least one other person, Natalie was sure.

Natalie carefully choose three entries for each group—floribundas, hybrid teas and grandifloras—and placed them in the cans. She leaned over, closed her eyes, and let the heady aromas drift up to her nostrils. A deep red rose, almost black, was the strongest. An apricot floribunda gave off a light, fruity scent. A yellow Peace hybrid reminded her of bath powder.

The fairgrounds were easy to find. Signs pointed the way, and the gate was open to exhibitors. She drove past the grandstand where horse races would be held daily, past several large exhibition halls that looked like airplane hangers. Workers on ladders washed windows. Vendors struggled to set up stands on a long parkway. At one end stood a half-erected ferris wheel without seats. She asked directions to the flower exhibits from a young girl leading a stubborn milk cow on a rope. Outside the glass front of the long, yellow exhibit building, two small children played on a lawn bordered with bright red geraniums.

Natalie parked her van by a side door and carried the box of roses inside. The place was enormous. People wearing nametags bustled about, looking official. Children raced back and forth. Multi-colored quilts and afghans hung on the walls. The stage held woodcraft items, dressers, chairs, a handmade cradle. One side of the large room was filled with clothing: sweaters, dresses and aprons. A huge display counter of preserves stood in the middle, a multi-colored pyramid. Quarts of pickles, fruits and vegetables stood on the lower shelves, pints and half-pints of jams and jellies at the top. A pack of cub scouts worked to set up Civil War dioramas in a corner, their progress impeded each time a new weapon or uniform was unpacked from a box. Matronly women stationed here and there on the main floor attempted to manage the disorder. A small group of people stood beside a glass bakery case watching a man with a discriminating countenance taste pies. The serious faces could have been watching a tricky procedure in neurosurgery.

She located the rose display in a corner of the room. As she stood there, holding the box of flowers, a perky woman in a print dress approached her with a smile.

"Hello," the woman said in a chirpy voice. "I just need your name. We have the labels already typed up."

"These are for Harriet Frazier."

The woman smiled again, walked back to her table and looked through a recipe box. She came back with several neatly typed labels, handed them to Natalie, and pointed to three long tables covered with white butcher paper. "Place your roses beside others of the same type. We'll check to make sure they're grouped properly. You'll find water in the restroom."

She peered more closely at the flowers. "Oh, dear," she said. "We mustn't have buds on the floribundas."

She took a small pair of pruning shears from the pocket of her smock and expertly snipped off a bud. "You must be new at this," she said, smiling again.

Natalie nodded and crossed the room to the opposite corner where a sign said "Restrooms." On her way back, she spotted Carol Bergstrom making a space on the pyramid for a jar of peaches. Carol looked up, returned Natalie's glance. A worried look spread across Carol's face. Had Natalie really frightened Carol with her threat of a lawsuit?

As Natalie was arranging the roses, someone tapped her on the shoulder. She turned and found herself staring at Carol.

"Miss Hughes, I want apologize for that piece in the paper. I shouldn't have included your name with Fishhawk's."

"I lost my job because of your article," Natalie said, clenching her fist. Her whole body grew tense. She felt like slapping Carol. "And I suspect there's some kind of conspiracy to frame Henry. I'm not leaving until I find the will, job or no job. I'll have more time to look for

it now."

Carol watched, saying nothing, as Natalie placed the last rose, a bright pink floribunda, next of one of Carol's that looked puny by comparison. Natalie smiled smugly as she turned back to Carol.

"I wish we could be friends," Carol said suddenly. "We were both close to Harriet." She stood awkwardly for a moment, wringing her hands and glancing around, then abruptly took Natalie's arm and led her out the door.

Opposite the exhibition hall stood the livestock barns. Through the wide side entrance Natalie saw enormous, doe-eyed milk cows lying on beds of straw, tended by 4-H children dressed in white slacks and shirts with green neckerchiefs.

"Theresa is here with a heifer she raised," Carol said. "Can I show it to you?"

"Maybe some other time," Natalie said, gently pulling her arm from Carol's grasp. What was it Carol didn't want her to see in the exhibition hall? "I have to be going."

Carol smiled, a shallow, weak smile, and opened her mouth to say something. Natalie turned and walked away.

Natalie circled around to the side entrance where her van was parked. She peeked in through the door and watched Carol disappear into a kitchen area where young 4-H girls were decorating a refreshment stand. Natalie walked among the displays, examined several afghans and embroidered pillows. Suddenly she remembered what had bothered her that morning in the master bedroom. Before Harriet's death there had been a quilt on the bed, covered with a white crocheted afghan. She didn't remember the pattern on the quilt, but she was sure it had been removed.

The walls of the hall were decorated with brightly colored quilts. Natalie's stomach grew tight as her gaze searched the wall around one side of the room, stopping momentarily to study each patchwork of art. Then she saw it. The quilt hung above the doorway where she had come in. Bordered in blue and green, with a centerpiece of a Great Blue Heron against a background of cattails.

Chapter Twenty-One: Conspiracy

Natalie's pulse pounded in her throat. She walked slowly up to the quilt and examined the label: The Blue Heron, Harriet Frazier. Auction item No. 48.

A tall, thin woman with a pleasantly aloof smile approached her.

"Can you tell me about the auction?" Natalie asked.

The woman's smile turned warm and friendly. "Oh, yes. It's for the Bingle family. They lost their house in a fire last May. Daughters of the Golden West are holding an auction tomorrow at three to raise money."

"I see. What about this quilt?"

"That will be auctioned. It's a lovely piece, don't you think? It should fetch at least two hundred dollars. So nice of Mrs..." She looked quickly at the label. "Mrs. Frazier to donate it."

"Do the items stay here until the fair is over?"

"We make exceptions if someone lives out of town. But we like to keep the exhibits together until the last day."

"Are there security guards on duty?"

The woman's smile waned and her face took on a puzzled look. "Several security guards patrol the grounds at night. We also have a new alarm system in the building."

"Thank you," Natalie said, turning to leave.

Natalie called Buck Davis from a pay phone outside the exhibition hall. Someone in his office took the call. Davis was in court testifying in another murder case, but the officer assured her the message would be relayed.

She hung up the phone and stood thinking, watching a pair of men unload a sorrel racehorse from a trailer. Should she stay here? There was really nothing she could do but wait for Buck to contact her. Carol Bergstrom obviously had figured out where the will was hidden. But Natalie doubted if Carol would try to steal it with so many people around, especially while one of the fair matrons was guarding it.

Should she alert the fair officials that an important piece of evidence in a murder case was hanging on a wall in their exhibition hall? What if the Bergstroms' influence extended to the County Fair officials? It was a tight-knit community of farmers and ranchers. And everyone who had known Harriet, or knew the Bergstroms, probably knew about the importance of finding—or destroying—the new will. Better not to trust anyone but Buck. Wasn't that what he had cautioned her? The most likely scenario was that the Bergstroms would try to purchase the quilt at the auction, which meant the will was safe for the time being. She thought about telling Helen, but could she trust her?

Natalie's mind raced as she drove back along the highway and turned off at Schooner Bluff Road. She felt tense and irritable, unable to focus. She drove around the bay, searching for the injured pelican she had seen before.

The pelicans could usually be found fishing from old pilings near the narrow mouth of the bay, where the water channeled through the jaws of two long, concrete breakwaters. Today, the pelicans were gone.

Natalie went back to the farm and hiked down to the slough to search the inner backwaters in her kayak. After two hours of paddling, she gave up and pulled the kayak out of the water. Maybe some Tai Chi would help calm her nerves; it had been days since she had last practiced. She found a flat place on the grass. In the middle of the warm ups, she faltered in the kicks. She repeated them, bringing each leg up separately in a counterclockwise arch to tap her toes with outstretched hands. She slowed her breathing and let her mind empty.

The sequence had a hundred movements, each flowing into the next. She breathed deeply, hands and arms moving slowly through the air as if pushing invisible clouds around her head. She bent her knees more, felt her back straighten, lifted her chin, felt her focus return.

This particular sequence was the long Wu form, brought from China by her teacher, Adrian Ching-Hua. She remembered Adrian's high-pitched voice admonishing her. "Stop waving your arms around like a ballet dancer! This is a martial art, not the Bolshoi."

Natalie lost her balance in the leg lifts. She stopped, kicked off her shoes, and wriggled her toes on the grass. The second time through, her balance was perfect.

Her mind ceased its chatter. She was in the moment, smelling the damp earth of the slough, watching a dunlin poking in the mud, framing the instant between her two hands, snaking down on one leg. It was always the same. By the time she finished, her body tingled with energy, her mind clear.

She stood with her hands on her hips, looking out over the bay. A line of pelicans flew by, disappeared into a backwater where she had never seen them before. She jumped into the kayak and paddled to the mouth of the little slough. The injured bird floated on the water, not thirty yards away. Seeing her approach, the bird threaded his way between the branches of willow and alder hanging over the muddy water and disappeared. It would be impossible to reach him until the tide was completely out, maybe in another hour.

Her stomach growled. It would remain light for several hours. She decided to go back to the farm and eat, try to reach Davis one more time, then return to catch the pelican.

It was five when Natalie reached the Blue Heron. A number of cars were parked outside: Helen's BMW, Richard's Mercury, two of the Bergstroms' vehicles, Ron's old truck. Someone must have called a meeting. It wasn't hard to guess why—Carol had located the mysterious "blue heron," and they were gathering to form a plan.

Skirting the house behind the rhododendrons, she quietly opened the back door and sneaked into the kitchen. Sophie woke up from napping in her basket and whined. Natalie whisked the little dog out the back door before she could bark, the stepped back inside and shut Sophie out. Voices carried from the living room. She tiptoed into the hallway to listen.

"...everyone will benefit. The development will only take up two hundred acres, with access to the highway. Since it's been drained for over fifty years, it doesn't qualify under Section 404 as a wetlands, except for a few months during the rainy season." Richard's voice was authoritative and assured. He seemed to be standing in the middle of the living room. "But we should move quickly. The Corps of Engineers are cracking down on developments near seasonal wetlands. I'm not worried about pushing this through in the next few months, but if we have to wait a year there could be trouble."

"You need an environmental impact report." Ron's voice was nearer, just inside the door. "It's next to a game refuge. You're talking about sewer systems, power lines-"

"I've handled all that," his father said.

"And the rest will be left for pasture?" Jack was farther away, by the french doors.

"That's right. Harriet let most of it go wild, but it shouldn't be wasted. Ten acres can be sold along with the houses. The bed and breakfast alone is worth quite a bit as a business. I don't suppose you two would be interested?"

"Possibly. It depends on the terms," Carol responded. Her voice came from near the spot where Jack must have been standing.

“What about the sale to the tribe?” Ron said.

“Well, that’s something we’ll need to decide. Once we destroy the will, we can terminate the escrow.”

“So what we're planning here is a conspiracy to thwart Harriet's last wishes,” Ron said.

“It's better than having to go to court and testify she was crazy,” his father snapped.

“That might be hard to prove.” Ron's voice was defiant.

“Not at all.” Richard sounded angry. “The oncologist told us about all the painkillers she was taking. That would certainly cloud a person’s judgment.”

“Harriet wasn't using drugs. The prescription bottles were practically full. They probably gave her side effects, and she was too stubborn to live like that.”

“Are you saying you won't testify if we need you, Ron?” Richard asked.

“I thought you were on our side.” Natalie recognized Theresa's high-pitched voice. She seemed to be standing close to Ron. The group was silent for a moment.

“I'm not sure I want to be included in this.” Helen spoke clearly and resolutely. “Mother came to see me two weeks ago. She was trying to make peace. She didn't tell me about the cancer, but at least she was making an effort to... to resolve things. I think we owe it to her memory to see her last wishes fulfilled.”

Again there was silence in the room.

"If you'll give me a few weeks, Helen, I can buy out your share," Richard said. "I'll be getting money from my backers as soon as the permits are issued. The best move would be to form a corporation and be partners, but if that doesn't appeal to you..."

"Oh, it appeals to me. I could practically retire on what we would make, if I invested wisely. But I have misgivings about selling out."

"It'd be the first time." Sheila was there. Her voice came from across the room, low and bitter.

"Let's try to be a family, why don't we?" Richard's voice was patronizing. His wife didn't answer. He continued. "If you want to make an issue of it, Helen, go ahead, but you'll have to fight me."

Sophie scratched at the back door and barked. There was an abrupt silence in the living room. Natalie slid out of the hallway into the kitchen and opened the door. Ron peeked in from the hallway, and Natalie avoided his surprised stare, hoping he would believe she had just walked in.

"Hi," she said lightly. "I saw all the cars parked outside. Are you having some kind of meeting?"

He seemed relieved she hadn't heard the conversation. "I wanted to talk to you, Nat." He pulled out a chair and sat down. Obviously he didn't want her to walk down the hallway toward the living room.

"Maybe you can begin by telling me why you lied to me about the pot."

He held a finger to his lips, signaling her to be quiet. “So that was you at the tent. I thought Waldo was acting funny. I took it for safekeeping, Nat. You know it was too valuable to leave lying around. Besides, it belongs to my family. You can hardly call that stealing.”

She relaxed a little. “No, I suppose not. But why didn't you tell me?”

“Because you would have told Buck.”

“So?”

“Don’t you think it would have made me look bad?”

She wanted to believe him, but she had lost trust. “So why didn't you tell me who Allison was?”

He looked up at her. She couldn't read his face. Calculating? Hurt? “I don’t think either of us drank enough to start sharing life stories.” He sounded irritated.

Theresa walked into the kitchen. Seeing Natalie, she flashed an angry look that quickly became a shallow smile. How much like her mother she was sometimes.

“Hello, Natalie. Would you like some coffee? I just made a pot. I can heat it back up.”

“Not right now, but I might take some with me in a thermos later.” Natalie turned to Ron. “Can we talk some other time? I have to eat and get back out on the bay.”

He raised one hand in a show of indifference. “Sure. Any time.” He stood up and walked out the door.

Natalie made a sandwich and went up to her room. The voices in the living room had moved out through the hallway. She peeked out the window and saw Helen and Richard talking heatedly outside, while the Bergstroms and Sheila stood back and watched. Ron was gone.

Twenty minutes later, Natalie heard tires crunching gravel in the driveway as the conspirators left, one by one. She wondered why Helen hadn't bothered to talk to her. Natalie tried to call Buck one more time, but he had left for home. The officer on the other end couldn't tell her if Davis had received her earlier message. She tried his beeper, then remembered seeing it once on the seat of his car. He didn't like to carry it. She called Buck's house and got his wife, Marie. Marie said she would have him call back as soon as he arrived.

She waited half an hour, then walked outside to look at the bay. The tide was out. She kept thinking about the pelican, her medicine bird. It was dying. She couldn't abandon it now. Surely the quilt would be safe for a few hours, until she reached Buck and asked him to secure it. After all, Richard's plan was to buy it at the auction, not steal it, and the auction was tomorrow.

Natalie went back downstairs to heat the coffee.

Chapter Twenty-Two: Rescue

Natalie packed a Swiss army knife, Snickers bar, and a small fishing net in her backpack, then glanced up at the clock. It was already past six, more than an hour after low tide. She would have to move quickly before the tide flowed back in over the mudflats; it would be almost impossible to capture the pelican from the kayak. A fog bank lurked darkly offshore, and she grabbed a slicker before putting on boots.

She pulled the kayak through shallow water at the slough until it was deep enough to hold her weight and clear the bottom. Common sense and all her training told her not to go alone, especially with such a large bird. But stubbornness and anger prevailed. There was no one left to trust.

Just enough water remained in the narrow channels to maneuver the kayak between the exposed mudflats. She paddled to the opening of the backwater where she had seen the injured pelican, but the other pelicans were gone and she saw no sign of the sick bird. Tired and frustrated, she stopped paddling and drifted. She poured a cup of coffee. It was still hot, but bitter enough to make her shudder. No wonder there had been half a pot left. She stirred it with the Snickers bar and took bites between sips.

As she sat, staring listlessly, she saw the pelican floating motionless near the bank. She poured the rest of the cup of coffee back into the thermos, the paddled quietly toward the pelican. He swam back into the undergrowth of willows and alder. Natalie followed, bending over to avoid the dangling branches. The pelican stopped where the bank curved inward to form a narrow bay. It was a perfect place to trap him.

She pulled the net from her pack and tied the kayak to the branch of a leaning alder, using it to form a barricade. She stuffed her shoes into the pack and pulled on the boots. Stepping out of the kayak into the shallows, she sank into mud up to her knees. She pulled her foot out and lost a boot in the oozing sludge. The pelican watched calmly.

Natalie took off the remaining boot, rolled up her pant legs, and peeled off her socks. She walked barefoot into the shallow water, her feet sucking at the mire with each step. After an eternity of advancing in slow motion toward the pelican, trying to find a firm foothold, she gave up on grabbing him. She was close enough to use the net, at least. The pelican had retreated to a mud bank out of the water. She tossed the net over his head, but he flapped out and slipped back onto the water.

Natalie gathered the net up and circled around onto the bank, slinking through the bulrushes and tall grass. As she approached from the opposite side, the pelican flapped further away and watched her warily. She was getting nowhere.

A giant alder leaning out over the water above gave her an idea. If she moved slowly, she might be able to climb out onto it and drop the net. The pelican seemed tired, closing his eyes for a moment. She hoped he had used the last of his strength.

Natalie's feet were numb from cold, making it difficult to balance. She slung the net over her shoulder and inched her way up the mossy trunk, over the slough. The pelican seemed unaware of her, and she stopped to rest her head. For a moment, she felt as if she might fall asleep in the tree with her face against the cool, green moss. She jerked her head up with a start. The pelican saw the movement and began to paddle away.

She threw the net perfectly over the pelican. He thrashed wildly, but remained stuck. She jumped down from the tree, slipped, and splashed backward into the water and mud. She staggered to her feet, covered in slime, and darted over to the struggling pelican. She grabbed his wings, but he swung his sharp-hooked beak around and made a quick thrust at her face. The beak missed her left eye by inches, hitting her shoulder and tearing her skin through the shirt. She flinched, almost dropping the pelican, then pinned his wings against his sides and picked him up.

The pelican went limp in her arms.

Natalie caught her breath, wondering if he had died from the shock. Then the pelican squirmed in her grasp, and she hurried over to the kayak. She tied the ends of the net together and put him on the seat, then took out her knife and cut the fishing line from his neck. The line had cut a deep, ugly wound that oozed pus and blood. She would have to take him in for treatment.

She moved him to the front of the kayak and tied the net down, then climbed into the seat, shivering uncontrollably. Natalie wondered if she had the strength to make it back. Her shoulder was bleeding, her clothes soaked and filthy, and all she wanted was to sleep.

She brought out the thermos and poured a cup of coffee. The hot liquid burned her throat as she gulped it down. The dregs were even more bitter than the first cup had been. It should have perked her up, but after waiting a few minutes for the caffeine to take effect, she only felt worse. The pelican writhed and knocked his head against the side of the kayak. She pulled him towards her and wedged the lower half of his body between her knees, then paddled laboriously out of the backwater. The weight of the kayak dragged on the water as if she paddled through sand.

After ten minutes she had only moved a few yards into the bay. A chill fog was blowing in from the sea, water droplets condensing on her hair and eyelashes. Her shoulder throbbed horribly. She felt suddenly dizzy, leaned over the side and vomited.

This wasn’t fatigue. The coffee's bitterness—someone had drugged her. With her last bit of strength, she pulled the rain slicker out of her pack and put it on, speaking aloud to herself.

"Slowly," she said. "First one arm then the other." Her voice sounded slurred.

The pelican wriggled suddenly, and she pulled him to her chest, weaving her arms through the net to keep him from falling over the wide. As she did so, the paddle slipped into the water and floated away. She closed her eyes and slid lower into the kayak until her head rested on the back of the seat.

When she opened her eyes her again, they were far out into the bay, drifting toward the mouth and the ocean beyond. She couldn't move. Her arms were lead weights hanging from the net. A chugging sound rose behind her, and she struggled to turn her head and look. A freighter carrying a load of logs tore through the fog, headed for the opening to the sea. The white lettering on the side of the giant black hull read Tonaka. The prow cut the water into twin gouts as the freighter moved straight toward the kayak.

She tried to speak, to cry out, but couldn't summon the strength. She closed her eyes again. Drifting in and out of sleep she felt the weight of the bird on her chest, then dreamed.

It was a dream of flight. Of lightness and elegance. Of powerful wings and a cold, pale blue sky. A line of pelicans skimmed the troughs between the waves. At first she was only one bird following the others. Then she knew they were united in the synchronism of flight, not separate, but one. As the leader flapped and glided, each bird followed, passing the movement through the line in a wavelike motion. She felt free and light, carried farther and farther from the drifting kayak and the heaviness of death.

Chapter Twenty-Three: Awaken

Natalie opened her eyes to a faint light in the dark distance. Her shoulder throbbed, but she was warm and dry. Someone or something breathed heavily beside her. She drifted back into a deep sleep. The next time she opened her eyes, she saw the dim outline of a window. Someone grabbed her wrist. She wrenched it fearfully away and looked up into the kind face of a white-capped nurse.

"Just taking your pulse, dear. I'm glad to see you're awake—we were worried about you for a while there, but you'll be all right now. Your pulse is back to normal. Would you like something to eat or drink? Maybe some juice or coffee?"

Coffee! The very thought made her ill. She suddenly remembered the bay and the pelican. She had been semi-conscious, adrift in a luminous haze. A dark hull had appeared above her. There were voices; someone had pulled her up by the armpits. More people shouting. Then she was rising into the air, up and up to the whirring of wings. The pelicans had carried her away.

Her shoulder ached. She gently prodded where the padded bandage hid the wound. She shuddered, remembering the cold, and turned her head. There, in a chair, sat Buck Davis, head tilted back, mouth hanging open as he softly snored.

"He's been here all night," the nurse said as Natalie turned back to her. "At first I thought he was your father. Said whatever happened was his fault—he shouldn't have left you there, whatever that means.

He's been holding your hand and rubbing it, talking to you. You were incoherent, chattering about birds—a blue heron, a pelican."

Natalie reached over and patted Buck's hand.

"Buck," she said gently.

He snorted, grabbed the arms of the chair, and looked around wide-eyed.

"Nat! Thank God you're awake. I heard them bring you in on the scanner. I drove out to the Frazier farm yesterday after dinner. I'd just gotten back in the car when it came over the radio. It didn't take much to put two and two together—an unconscious woman in a kayak with an injured pelican. How many people could that be?"

She smiled, tried to sit up. A wave of dizziness crashed over her and she lay back down. "What happened to the pelican? Is he still alive?"

"Yes. He's fine. The Coast Guard took him to the Wildlife Care Center. He saved you, you know."

"The pelican?"

"Your pulse was faint when they found you. Hypothermia. The pelican was on top of you. I guess you were holding him pretty tightly. He kept you warm enough, even though you were soaked to the bone."

"I was drugged, Buck. Someone laced my coffee. I don't remember much at all after putting on my slicker. Who found me?"

"A boy on a pilot boat was watching a line of pelicans and spotted your kayak below them."

A dream of wings, thought Natalie. "What time is it?"

Buck tilted his wrist to check his watch. "Almost noon."

"Did you get the will?"

"The will?"

She sat up abruptly, fighting the urge to vomit. "The quilt! It's being auctioned. Didn't you get my message?"

"What message?"

Natalie groaned. "I left a message yesterday! Someone in your office said they'd get it to you."

His face grew serious. "What about the will?"

She told him briefly about the quilt, the auction, and the conspiracy to destroy the will. "I thought that was why you were at the Blue Heron last night."

"No. I was going to see Mary Slocum, and I stopped to bring you along. Thought she might prefer to talk to you. Do you have any idea who drugged your coffee?" Buck asked.

"Ron or Theresa. I'm sure of it. They were the only ones who knew I was going to heat it back up and drink it later."

The nurse came in with a lunch tray. Natalie stuffed fruit and a chicken sandwich down between gulps of milk. A few minutes later she pushed the tray away and threw off the covers.

"If you'll excuse me, I need to get dressed."

"In what?"

"Oh, God. I forgot. My clothes were ruined."

"I think you should stay here. I have plenty of time to make it to the fairgrounds before the auction."

"I'm going if I have to hitchhike in this hospital gown. I feel better now that I've eaten." She sat up on the side of the bed and stretched a foot to the floor. Her head ached horribly and the room spun.

"All right!" Buck said. "I see that nothing I can say will keep you here. Let me know what size you are, and I'll get some clothes. We can drop by Slocum's on our way to the fair. We still have plenty of time."

She gave him her shirt, slacks, and shoe size. Twenty minutes later he was back with a large shopping bag from a local department store.

"I gave the clerk your sizes and she picked out some stuff. I told her you probably needed underwear, too."

In the bathroom Natalie examined the new outfit: jeans, a red cotton turtleneck, socks, a pair of pull-on canvas shoes, a bra a size too small and underpants. She felt weak, and her shoulder hurt. She wondered if she had the energy to go along. She might slow Buck down. Well, if so, she could drop out. She wanted to be there, needed to be there, when the quilt came down from the wall.

When she opened the door to the hospital room, the nurse was waiting with a clipboard full of papers and a pen.

"You need to fill out these forms, Miss Hughes."

"I have to leave right away. Is there a doctor around who can release me?"

"I don't know. I could check. Don't you think you should rest? You must still be weak."

"I can't. I have important business with a murderer."

Chapter Twenty-Four: Auction

Buck drove south on Highway 101 along the bay, headed for Schooner Bluff road.

"I still don't have it all figured out," he said. "I think Mary Slocum saw someone at Frazier's the day Mrs. Frazier was murdered and is covering for them. My guess is that it was Jack Bergstrom, but until I have her story, I can't really bring him in for questioning."

"What about the quilt?"

"We'll get it as soon as I talk to Mary. I bet Bergstrom is at the fair, and with so much at stake, I think he'll show up at the auction. I can question him there."

Twenty minutes later they pulled up in front of Mary Slocum's yellow mobile home. The door was locked. Inside, the dogs barked hysterically. Buck called to the back of the house, but there was no answer.

"She might be walking out on the bluff," Natalie said. "I can show you where."

The road ran along the bluff before angling down to the spit. Natalie spotted a brightly clad figure walking along the dunes, carrying a black trash bag. Davis stopped a few feet ahead of Mary, and Natalie leaned out the window.

"Mary. Can we talk to you a minute?"

The old woman wore a yellow windbreaker and red baseball cap. She leaned in at the window, and the smell of cigarettes on her breath made Natalie draw back.

"You can sit in the back if you'd like," Buck said.

"Am I under arrest?" Mary eyed him suspiciously.

"No, ma'am. I just thought you'd be more comfortable back there. I had something I thought you should see."

Buck handed a case file to Natalie, and she passed it out the window to Mary.

"We wanted you to see this," Natalie said. "It's the file on your son's murder. There was a cover up, Mary. The police knew all along who did it."

Mary squinted at the typewritten page, a look of shock slowly replacing her expression of suspicion. "Jack was the one who killed him?"

"It was an accident, so he wasn't charged. Helen was there. The families convinced the sheriff to keep their names out of it."

Mary spat on the side of the road, thrust the file back through the window. "All this time I thought he was helping out because he cared, but it was only guilt. He killed my sweet boy."

Buck cleared his throat. "Mrs. Slocum, we want to know what you saw the day Mrs. Frazier was murdered. Richard Frazier's car wasn't there that day, was it?"

"What will happen to me if… if you think I lied about it earlier?"

"Nothing, so long as you tell me the truth now."

"I need to sit down."

Natalie jumped out and opened the back door for the old woman. She sat heavily in the seat and breathed out a shuddering sigh. "I went to Mrs. Frazier's that day with some willow bark. She had real bad pain, said it was a bleeding ulcer. I gave her comfrey tea and aloe. She was real upset, didn't even invite me in."

"What time was that?" Davis asked.

"Maybe one. When I came back from my walk a couple hours later, I saw Jack driving away from her house. I wanted to protect him. I hate Richard Frazier, always did. Thought maybe he was the one killed Charley." She took out a cigarette and lit it. "I'll testify against Jack if you want me to, say whatever you want."

Buck and Natalie exchanged worried looks.

A line of cars inching forward on the two-lane highway leading to Fern Valley marked the entrance to the fairgrounds. Buck was quiet, driving with one hand, rubbing his chin, frowning. He had told the dispatcher to call the main office at the fairgrounds and send a security guard to the Home Crafts exhibition hall, where Buck would give further instructions. He ignored Natalie's sideways glances. Finally, she couldn't stand it any longer.

"So you're going to arrest Bergstrom?" she asked.

"I'm taking him in for questioning. We'll get the quilt and the will. But I still don't have enough to prove he did it. And any halfway decent attorney will tear Mary Slocum apart. She already lied once in an affidavit."

"I think I know what happened," Natalie said. "Bergstrom took the adze home with him after he killed Harriet, then conspired with Carol to plant it at Fishhawk's mobile."

"That's what I think, too, but there's no way to link him with the adze unless someone starts telling the truth or his fingerprints match the unknown latents we found. What about the attempt on your life, the drugged coffee?"

"Carol knew I was in the exhibition hall. She may have guessed I spotted the quilt. Theresa told her I was going to drink the coffee later, and Carol drugged it."

"She could only have done it while you were in your room after the meeting. I thought you said everyone left but Ron."

"You're right. I saw Carol outside, then she left."

"Then someone else must have used Mrs. Frazier's prescription drugs. There were sleeping pills in the medicine cabinet. We'll search the house later, see if we can turn up an empty plastic container."

"You still think Ron is a primary suspect, don't you?"

"I can't play favorites with suspects."

"But he was her grandson!"

"And a fifth of all premeditated murders are committed by members of the immediate family. I think you've been blinded to that possibility by his charm."

The angry tone of his statement came across like a slap in the face. She rolled down the window and stared out, her arms wrapped around her chest. Why was she defending Ron?

A white sheriff's deputy car was parked outside the main entrance. Buck signaled the deputy in the car to follow.

"Mackovich," he said to himself in a tone of disgust.

They found a parking space next to a wide gate with a "No Parking" sign, not far from the Home Crafts Hall. It was two o'clock.

"Do you remember a number on that quilt?" Buck asked Natalie.

"Forty-eight. It will take a while to get to it."

Davis opened the glove compartment and pulled out a shoulder holster with a revolver in it. Natalie saw another gun in the compartment, an automatic pistol. Davis reached under the seat for a box of bullets. He loaded the revolver, set the safety, took off his jacket, and put on the holster.

He looked up at Natalie's face and smiled reassuringly. "Just a precaution. We arm ourselves anytime we have to bring in a suspect. Supposed to wear it all the time I'm on duty, but I hate the sweaty thing."

The deputy stepped out of his patrol car and sauntered over to greet Davis, or at least attempted a saunter that quickly turned into a wobble. His small eyes peered out incuriously from a pudgy face split by a thick, dark mustache. "Buck. Ma'am."

A security guard appeared at the north side of the exhibition hall. He pulled out a ring of keys and unlocked the padlock holding the gate closed. A short, thin man with white hair dangling from the sides of his cap, his demeanor was serious but Natalie thought she could wrestle him to the ground in no time. She hoped there wasn't any trouble, because Buck's backup seemed about as capable as the local Garden Club.

Inside the exhibition hall, the auction was already in progress. The auctioneer, a gray-haired man in suspenders that seemed about to burst from the pressure of his enormous gut, stood on the stage pointing with one hand and holding a mike in the other. His rapid-fire exchange with the silent participants echoed through the building. Natalie guessed there were at least two hundred people seated on folding metal chairs. Others leaned against the walls. A number of onlookers milled about between the displays.

"The quilt is over there," she whispered, pointing to the opposite doorway.

"Why, there's Miss Hughes and Mr. Davis!" They turned to see Carol Bergstrom and Theresa, leading a spotted tan and white milk cow toward the building.

Buck bent his head toward the security guard and spoke softly. "Go stand by that quilt with the blue heron on it, to the left of the far entrance, and don't let anyone touch it or take it down. It has an important piece of evidence inside. Get the number and have one of the fair attendants tell the auctioneer to take it off the list. I'll be back in a minute."

He turned to Carol and nodded.

"I want to talk to Jack, Mrs. Bergstrom. Where can I find him?"

Theresa's eyes grew wide. Carol nudged her. "You stay here, Theresa. I'm going to find your dad."

Buck and Mackovich followed Carol as she headed toward the livestock barns.

"What's going on?" Theresa asked.

"They want to question your father about where he was the day Harriet was murdered," Natalie said.

Theresa shuddered and tears appeared in her eyes. "They know he was there that day, don't they?"

"Mary Slocum saw him leave." Natalie put an arm around the girl. "Come sit down with me. We can talk." Theresa waved at another teenager, a girl with red hair and freckles and a white 4-H shirt.

"Jody," Theresa said. "Would you hold my heifer while I talk to Miss Hughes a minute?"

Jody looked sympathetic. "Sure, Theresa. What's wrong?"

"Nothing." She wiped her eyes and handed the rope to the other girl. "Just be careful—she's skittish around so many people."

Jody took the rope and pulled the reluctant heifer toward the entrance to the cattle barn. A moment later, Buck stepped out with Carol and Jack.

"We need to know why you lied about Mary Slocum leaving the Frazier house around the time of the murder," Buck said. "We're not pressing charges right now, but I want a full written statement from you, and it's going to take some time."

Jack Bergstrom looked shaken, defeated. "I was there that day. But Harriet was still alive when I left. I swear it."

"We'll need to take your fingerprints as well," Buck said, continuing as if Jack had said nothing. "It might look better if you came in on your own and made a statement."

Jack looked first at Carol, then Theresa. Carol seemed in shock, pale, hands trembling. He put an arm around her shoulders. "Don't worry, hon. Everything's going to be all right. I didn't kill Harriet Frazier." He took a step toward Theresa, and she backed away from him.

"Mackovich will take you in to headquarters," Buck said. "I'll be along in a few minutes."

Mackovich led Jack away. Carol shot Natalie a furious look, then turned to Theresa, who was sobbing.

Carol put an arm around her daughter's shoulders. "I'll take care of auctioning Scooter. You're in no condition."

Theresa nodded. Carol patted her on the back and hurried over to the cattle barn.

Natalie put an arm around Theresa and led her into the exhibition hall. They sat on a bench against one wall as Buck spoke quietly to the security guard. The guard hurried into another room, came back with a ladder, and climbed up to take the quilt off the wall.

As the auctioneer reeled off the bids on a handmade rocking horse, Natalie saw Richard Frazier rise from a front row seat and walk toward Buck. She spotted Helen standing across the room, Ron beside her. They were all watching the guard take the quilt down. None of them seemed to have noticed Natalie yet.

Sheila appeared in the side entrance, then followed Richard as he approached Buck with an angry expression. Although Natalie couldn't hear their exchange, she saw the tension in their faces and postures. Sheila stood behind Richard, arms crossed.

Theresa was saying something, almost incoherent with sobs. Natalie nodded, still watching Buck and Richard, paying little attention. Then she heard something that made her stiffen.

"It's all my fault," Theresa sobbed. "I told him Harriet was changing the will that day. And then when I found her, I took the adze."

"What?" Natalie said, her full attention on Theresa.

"I heard Harriet tell Fishhawk on the phone that morning about the new will. At first I didn't know whether to tell Dad, 'cause I knew he'd be furious, and we were busy moving the cattle between pastures. When I did tell him, he jumped in the truck and drove off.

"I waited for him to come back, but when he didn't, I rode my horse over to Harriet's. I found her there, with the blood, and the adze—"

Theresa took a deep, shuddering breath, then continued.

"I thought he did it, that his fingerprints were on it, so I rolled it up in a towel and took it home."

"You planted it at Fishhawk's?"

"I'm sorry, I'm so sorry. It was Ron's idea." She looked up at Natalie, fear in her eyes. "At first I hid the adze behind some bales of straw in the barn. I didn't know what to do with it. Dad came home later, and he'd been drinking. I told him what I saw. That was after I talked to you. He was totally shocked. He said I mustn't tell anyone he'd gone over to talk to her. He swore she was alive when he left her. I didn't know whether to believe him or not. It was driving me crazy. I knew I had to get rid of the adze, but I didn't know where to hide it. I took it to Ron and told him the whole story."

"And he hatched the plan to frame Fishhawk? You were the one who called the sheriff with the tip about where to find the murder weapon?"

"I was," Theresa said, and shuddered again. "Ron said it would save my father, and the farm. If everyone thought it was Fishhawk, the Fraziers could back out of the land deal."

Natalie remembered Ron staring at the spot of blood on the floor next to Harriet's dead body, then looking through the rooms. Could it possibly be that he knew the adze had been there and was missing? Was he really checking to see if it had been moved, instead of looking for missing possessions?

Any reasonable person would have gone to the sheriff with Theresa's evidence. Any reasonable person would want the real murderer brought to justice. Unless he knew for sure Bergstrom wasn't the real murderer.

"I love him, you know," Theresa said.

Natalie put her hand on Theresa's shoulder, unsure what to say, but Theresa shrugged it away and ran crying from the building.

Natalie stood, staring at nothing. Ron had snowed her, too. She thought of when he came looking for her the day of the murder. It wasn't a coincidence—he wanted an alibi. Someone to be with him when he pretended to discover the body, the whole thing staged to make her believe in his innocence. And then when he discovered Harriet had written a new will and hid it, he had tried to get close to Natalie, to seduce her like he had seduced Theresa.

She looked across the room at Ron. He was staring at her. Had he seen Theresa talking to Natalie? In that moment she was sure. Sure he had killed Harriet. Sure he had drugged her coffee. She stiffened, stared back, an angry, icy stare. He turned away and watched the security guard slowly climbing down the ladder with the quilt in his arms.

A loud bellow made Natalie start. Theresa's heifer crashed into the hall, knocking over tables and chairs. Women screamed and grabbed their children. Carol ran past, not after the heifer, but toward the opposite entrance, where the security guard stood on the ladder. He held the quilt folded over one arm.

A group of men sprang into action to corner the heifer. Frightened, with nowhere to go, it hurled itself toward an old farmer in overalls. He put out his arms and yelled, "Hey!" The heifer swerved away, crashing into a pyramid of preserves. The mason jars, open for tasting, toppled over and spilled their contents across the floor. A crowd had gathered along the walls of the hall, some standing and watching, others pushing toward the exits, blocking any chance for the heifer to move outside. People stomped over the spilled food, squashing peaches, pickles and tomatoes underfoot. The acrid odor of vinegar wafted through the air.

The guard holding the quilt moved back up the ladder to watch the fracas from a safer location. Ron walked to the ladder. Buck, standing nearby, moved to intercept him.

Ron shoved the ladder over, and guard and ladder toppled toward Buck. Buck dodged the ladder and caught the guard, cushioning his impact, but both were knocked sprawling. Richard darted out from the crowd along the wall and grabbed the quilt off the floor before Ron could pick it up.

Richard ran for the wide main doors, but they were blocked by a scrum of people either trying to get out and away from the chaos or trying to get in to see what was happening. He changed direction and ran across the empty center of the building, toward the exit on the far side, but Helen and Carol intercepted him. Both grabbed a corner of the quilt. Richard slipped and fell on the preserves, still holding the quilt.

The women tore frantically at the cloth patchwork and the quilt came apart in seconds. Carol yanked a piece of paper from the centerpiece. Natalie ran toward her, shoving people out of the way. Ron ran at them from the other side and Buck staggered after him.

Someone yelled, "Watch out!" The heifer broke through a ring of men around her. She bellowed and charged for the center of the room, head down, at a mother pulling her small child toward the exit. Buck, a few feet away, saw the danger and shoved the mother and child out of the way a split second before the heifer reached them. The heifer tried to jump over Buck, but one hoof caught him in the chest.

Buck cried out, grimacing with pain. The animal swerved, headed off in another direction. The child crouched screaming under a table, her mother trying to pull her back out. Buck lay on the floor, unmoving.

"Stop him, he's got the will!" Helen screamed.

Glancing in the direction Helen pointed, Natalie saw Ron heading for the doorway, a piece of paper in his hand. Natalie looked around frantically for the security guard. He sat on the floor next to the wall, looking stunned and rubbing his ankle.

The heifer barreled back from the front of the hall, eyes wide, scattering onlookers in her path, then veered off and headed toward the north entrance. Several people made way for the cow and it ran outside, heading toward the livestock barns. Natalie ran to Buck. His eyes were open, staring at the ceiling. He didn't seem to be breathing. Blood seeped through his shirt.

Buck rolled his eyes toward Natalie. A young man shoved his way through the crowd and knelt at Buck's side.

"I'm a doctor," he said. "What happened?"

Everyone spoke at once. The young doctor unbuttoned Buck's shirt to look at his injury. "Someone call an ambulance," he said without looking up.

Buck took a short breath and winced. Natalie leaned down to whisper into his ear.

"Ron took the will. I'm going after him," she said. "Let me have your car keys."

He shook his head back and forth. She reached into his pant pocket and drew out the keys. A look of shock spread across his face, but he couldn't speak. For a moment she felt guilty, felt she should stay to be sure he was all right. But stronger than that was a growing feeling of rage and betrayal, a certainty that she had been duped from the moment of Harriet's death.

"Will he be okay?" she asked the doctor.

"He's had the wind knocked out of him. Maybe broken ribs. He's not going to die."

Natalie stood up. Buck tried to raise his hand, a signal for her to wait. She ignored him and rushed out the side entrance, hoping she wasn't too late.

Chapter Twenty-Five: Revenge

Natalie unlocked Davis's car and sat in the driver's seat. She examined the radio, pushed some buttons, played with the dials, tried to get the mike to work. Nothing but static. She gave up after a few minutes. It was like a recurring nightmare, trying to dial for help but unable to get it right. She replaced the mike and considered calling the sheriff's department by phone. Surely someone else had already called.

Time was running out. Ron had a short lead. Every minute counted. If she called and the sheriff's department learned Buck was injured, they would probably send someone out to the fairgrounds first to confirm Natalie's story before following her directions. The department was notorious for their slow response to anything but a shooting. Even then, driving time was half an hour from Clam Beach.

She opened the glove compartment, pulled out the automatic pistol, checked the grip to see if there was a clip inside. It was empty. She reached beneath the seat, located a box with four clips, and took one out. Mark had bought an automatic pistol, a Smith and Wesson nine millimeter, when they were first married. He brought it home the day after a break-in at the apartment next door and kept the pistol buried in his sock drawer. He had shown her how to use it but, being Mark, he'd done it too quickly to follow and hadn't let Natalie load it herself.

She struggled to remember how it worked, pushing the clip into the opening in the grip until she felt it click. The weapon was heavy in her hand. It toppled the barriers of her rage, gave her the gift of power. The rush of adrenaline from holding it brought clarity and freedom from fear. She took a deep breath, laid the gun down on the seat.

She started the car and drove out the gate. A line of traffic backed up from the stop sign at the highway must have slowed Ron's progress. As she pulled onto the main thoroughfare, she saw his pickup in a line of cars heading up a slope in the distance. A traffic jam in the opposite lane made it impossible for her to pass, but at least she knew where he was headed. Ten minutes later, she saw him turn off onto Schooner Bluff road. She had to wait for a space in the oncoming traffic before she could turn off in pursuit. By then his truck had disappeared. A cloud of dust told her he was heading for the farm.

When Natalie arrived at the Blue Heron, Ron's truck was parked in the driveway. If he was inside, he would have heard the car, would be waiting for her. She hoped he had returned to his camp to retrieve the pot, but she played it safe. She sat waiting for a few minutes, watching the windows of the house for any sign of movement.

Finally, she opened the car door and slid out, crouched behind the rose bushes. She made her way across the yard to the old Victorian and quietly opened the screen door to the back porch, then tiptoed inside. She could hear her heart pounding. She kicked open the door to the kitchen, holding the gun in both hands, covered one room after another. The house was empty. He was at the dig.

As she walked through the pasture she alternately felt afraid and angry. She stopped once, wanting to turn back, forced herself to look out over the bay. She closed her eyes, imagined earth movers flattening the depressions that became ponds in the rainy season, thought of black Brant, marine geese, stopping here during their long migration between Baja and Alaska. The bay was a critical rest and feeding area for them, and all the bird species around the bay needed the shallow ponds on Harriet's pasture to reduce crowding and prevent another outbreak of avian cholera. If Ron destroyed the will, the birds would find only asphalt, lawn, and rooftops. They would circle in confusion, then fly away into oblivion.

As she hurried along the path, she knew she was probably too late, but she wanted to confront him. He had once told her he didn't own a gun. She hoped that, at least, had been the truth.

Waldo barked when he saw her. Ron peeked out of the tent, then came outside, looking wary. When she was a few yards away, she pulled out the gun and aimed it at him.

"Give me Harriet's will."

He looked shocked, then angry. "You're crazy. The will's in a safe place. All I was doing was getting it away from the family. They would have destroyed it."

"I want to see it."

He opened his mouth to speak, but she pointed the gun at his chest, "Now!"

He ducked to go back in the tent. She circled around to watch him through the opening. He reappeared, holding a piece of paper.

"Here," he said, thrusting it at her.

She was only a few feet away. "Crumple it up and throw it to me."

He looked exasperated, as if he were dealing with a petulant child, but did as he was told. She knelt, picked up the paper, and smoothed it out with one hand, keeping the gun pointed at him with the other. It was a standard form that Harriet had completed and signed. Henry's signature was above Duffy's. She stuffed it into her jacket.

Ron took a step toward her, and she thrust the gun out, still aiming it at his chest.

"Don't come any closer," she said.

She was shaking now, not sure if it was from fear or anger. Probably both. She stared at his face, studied the chiseled beauty, the dark eyes that had lured her to trust him. And suddenly she saw a different person. What she had mistaken for sensitivity and depth was really the look of a haunted child. He had received so little of what he needed to feel good about himself that he had developed an intense desperation, using deception simply to survive. She looked again. The pain and longing in his eyes was not what she had imagined it to be. He was not a survivor. His was a tortured soul, capable of justifying to himself the very worst acts.

Ron smiled. “Come on, Nat. Put the gun down. In the first place, it's dangerous. In the second, you're scaring me. You've got the will. I was going to take it to an attorney, anyway.”

“You killed her.”

“Harriet? Don't be stupid. Why would I kill Harriet?”

“Because you stood to inherit a lot of money someday. You found out she had cancer, and you didn't want the land deeded to someone else because you were close to discovering the burial cave. I may not have it all right, but I've figured out most of it.”

He gave her a blank stare, but she continued. “Harriet was going to an attorney the next day. You argued with her, and she stood her ground. You went into the Blue Heron, got the adze and killed her. You probably knew Fishhawk's prints were on it.”

“But you told me a woman called in the tip. How could it have been me?”

“Theresa told me how the two of you plotted to frame Fishhawk. Jack Bergstrom was at the house that afternoon. Theresa came later, found Harriet dead, and took the adze because she thought it would save her father. She made the mistake of telling you. But you were the one who killed Harriet.”

“That's a lie. Bergstrom killed her.”

“I'm supposed to believe that when Theresa brought you the murder weapon you hid it to protect Jack? No, you planned to blame

Fishhawk all along. Theresa interfered, then gave you the opportunity to carry out your original plan. It all fits together."

His face grew angry. "I've heard enough of this bullshit. Give me the gun." He walked toward her, his hand outstretched. "Come on, Nat. You can't shoot an unarmed man. I doubt if you could shoot an armed one."

He closed in on her. She steadied her aim. He stopped.

"I swear to God I'll shoot if you take one more step," she said.

He took a step.

She closed her eyes and pulled the trigger.

Nothing happened. He lunged at her, grabbed her wrist, twisted it until she cried out and dropped the gun. He shoved her backwards and she fell. Ron picked up the gun, worked the slide, and pointed it at her.

"You have to load the chamber first, Nat. Doesn't shoot otherwise."

Tears stung her eyes as she sat up. Her shoulder throbbed.

"Stand up," he said.

She stumbled to her feet.

"Give me the will."

She stared at him defiantly.

"You're right," Ron said. "I killed Harriet. And I'll kill you if you don't do what I say. Give me the will."

Chapter Twenty-Six: The Cave

Natalie handed the will to Ron. He walked backwards to the tent and pushed the piece of paper through a slit in the netting.

"Walk back up the path. I want to show you something—I found the cave. Waldo, stay!"

The dog reluctantly lay down beside the tent.

She walked along the path toward the ravine. He made her halt at the edge.

"Climb down to where that spruce root is sticking out," he ordered

As she made her way down the cliff, Natalie thought of letting herself fall. If she wasn't injured too badly, she could make out the bottom. The height didn't bother her, because the ravine was so grown together it was impossible to see down more than a few yards. But if she caught on a branch, he would have a chance to shoot.

She looked up to see him pointing the gun at her. When she reached the giant root, she held onto it and climbed lower.

"Stop there. Do you see anything?" At first she saw nothing. Then, as her eyes adjusted, she made out a hollow beneath the roots of the spruce.

"I brought Waldo up here. He found the place."

Three fox kits peered out at her from their den. They were huddled together, two behind a third, who showed his teeth fiercely as the other two shook with fright. Seeing their soft gray fur and small black eyes and noses, Natalie felt overwhelmed with tenderness. The roof of the den was hairy with spruce roots. Bone fragments lay strewn on the floor, next to a shape that might have been part of a human skull with chewed edges. On the back wall, black lines came together to make a shape.

"I think the walls have pictographs," Ron said, peering down at her, excitement in his voice. "They're incredibly rare in this part of California. Once it's dug out we'll know who lived here. That wall seems to have held pretty well, but the front of the cave fell and buried whatever was in there. We'll have to be careful removing the trees to give us access." His voice had changed, taken on an eerie tone, as if he were talking to himself. He still believed he could get away with it. "You can come back up now."

"Why did you show me this?"

"So you could see why I had to do it. Harriet wanted me to stop searching. After talking to Fishhawk, she got the wild idea that the burial cave was sacred—that it shouldn't be tampered with. We argued. That was the night before."

Natalie felt sick. She thought of the ravine bustling with loud people, excavating the bank, removing the spruce, taking the kits away. Was he deliberately tormenting her? He marched her back to the pasture, then out toward the bluff.

"I didn't really want to kill Harriet," he said. "I had to. She wouldn't listen to reason. She called at the beginning of summer, told me about the cancer. She didn't want to be alone the last months of her life, invited me to stay. Said I could search for the cave. I wasn't supposed to tell anyone about her cancer. Once I got here, she said she was considering changing the will, leaving everything to me and bypassing Helen and Dad. I was so excited." He looked off into the distance, toward the house.

Natalie watched the barrel of the gun, hoping he would lower it. But he held it tightly, pointed at her chest, and continued talking.

"Grandpa promised me for years that all the land would be mine someday. I dreamed about it. Then Harriet told me about the cave and the pot, and I realized what was here. This will cause a sensation. Don't you see the possibilities?"

"I see a greedy man who killed his grandmother because he was a failure in his own life. Because he wanted a free ticket to success."

"It was our secret! Harriet's and mine. I trusted her." His voice lowered, grew angry. "But she started talking to Fishhawk, going out to that rock, sitting there for hours, watching the birds. She said she had to give the land back—to the natives and the wildlife, make some kind of atonement. We argued. I tried to talk sense into her, but she was crazy. I could see it in her eyes, a faraway look, like I wasn't there. She told me to take the Anasazi pot and leave."

Natalie understood finally how it happened, the inevitability of Harriet's premature death. Harriet must have watched Ron, trying to decide if he would be a worthy steward of the land. And she began to see how greedy and immature he really was. It must have been hard. Her only grandchild, and she couldn't save him. Natalie felt weak and tired. She wondered how he planned to kill her, tried to think of how she could keep him talking while she planned some escape.

"So why didn't you take the pot and leave?" Natalie asked.

He looked down at her. "I was going to. I tried to convince her one more time, that afternoon."

"You had tea with her?"

"She said she'd made up her mind, seemed smug and self-satisfied, superior. I never guessed she'd already written the will, hidden it. I said good-bye and walked over to the display case to get the pot. I stood in the hall, looking around at the artifacts I was supposed to inherit. I had spent hours in there as a kid, taking stuff out, feeling it. It was my treasure, and she was giving it away! I didn't even have a place to go. My life had come to an end."

"That's when you saw the adze and got the idea to frame Henry. You remembered his fingerprints were on it."

"It would have worked!" he said.

"Except Theresa took the murder weapon and hid it, and you had to bring her into the conspiracy. She would have broken down sooner or later and told the truth. She's just a kid. Once there was any question about her father's guilt, she would have implicated you."

He stiffened. “There's nothing to prove I did it. It's just a guess. Don't make me choose between killing you and going to prison, Nat. I'll make a deal with you—”

“No deals, Ron. The best thing for you to do is turn yourself in.”

He looked astonished. “You're crazy. Can't you see why I had to kill her? She was dying. I did us both a favor. I saved her from a long, painful, ugly death.”

“It was murder, Ron. It was wrong.”

“It was a mercy.”

“What about the sedatives in my coffee? Was that supposed to be a mercy killing? I almost died out on the bay.”

“I didn't know you were going out in the kayak to drink it. It was supposed to knock you out for a few hours. I thought you would drink it the next morning.”

They stared at each other for a moment. He studied her face, then seemed to realize it was no good trying to convince her. He sighed. “I don't think I could put a bullet through your pretty head, Nat. Better that you have an accident. Start walking.” He gestured back toward the path through the pasture.

The fog was thick in low places, and they could barely see six feet in front of them. Most of the time they were completely hidden from the house. As she walked ahead of him, her feet felt leaden. Surely someone would come. Buck would send a deputy. Or Helen would be there, see Buck's car and come searching. They cut across the pasture to Spirit Rock. The fog thinned out close to the bluff, where the breeze sent the mists whirling upward like white feathers.

Natalie followed Ron's directions numbly as he led her to the edge of the rocks. She was overcome with fear and dizziness, confused. She closed her eyes briefly, steadied herself, vowed not to look down no matter what happened. When she opened her eyes, Ron was peering over the edge. Far below, the roar of waves pounding against giant rocks grew loud, then soft. She wanted to throw up. She knew it wasn't a straight shot down. A narrow ledge hugged the cliff ten feet below, hugging the edge of the bluff. If Ron planned to make it look like an accident, he had to shove her from the ledge and not the top.

"No one will believe I just happened to tumble off a cliff," she said.

"I'll tell them I came here, trying to decide what to do with the will, wrestling with my conscience. You followed me and we quarreled. You grabbed the will, ran back through the fog, and fell." He shrugged.

There was a place where the angle of the bluff made it possible to climb down to the ledge. He made her go first. Natalie breathed slowly, in and out, imagining she was doing a Tai Chi sequence. She felt the energy around her, drew it in through her body, imagined she was surrounded by a golden light. Her thoughts quieted. It steadied her, took her mind away from her fear and the sound of crashing waves. She studied the side of the cliff, focused on the intricate fractals of chiseled rock where tiny succulents grew.

Natalie looked for a solid handhold as she reached the ledge. Her right hand grasped a cleft in the rocks. She took one long breath and stood waiting. When he glanced down at the rocks to get his footing, she brought her leg up in a swift circular kick that caught him in the hip. He lost his balance. She kicked again. He nearly fell, his hand flying up, the gun sailing in an arc away from the cliff. He lunged forward and slipped, managed to grab her shoe with one hand as he slid over the edge, pulled her feet out from under her.

As she fell, she grabbed a jagged piece of the cliff. It cut into the palms of her hands. Ron hung from her shoe.

"Pull me up!" he cried.

She used her other foot to pry the shoe from her foot, thankful for Buck's choice of cheap slip-ons.

"No, Ron," she said. "You'll just try to kill me again, you son of a bitch."

The shoe came off.

She heard him slide down the cliff. Small rocks tumbled after him, tracing his fall.

Natalie sat there a few moments, overcome with nausea and dizziness, eyes closed, heart pounding. Once the vertigo subsided, she felt a sudden rush of relief. She let her head fall back on her shoulders and took a deep breath. Every part of her body seemed to be surging with energy. The mist brushed over her arms and face like soft feathers. Every sound around her was magnified—the surging waves, the circling seagulls. She had never felt so alive. She peered over the ledge to see where Ron had fallen, but the fog obscured the view. The dizziness returned. She rose, climbed to the top of the cliff, afraid to look down again, and staggered across the pasture.

Inside the tent, she found the will and stuck it in her jacket. Waldo followed her back to the Blue Heron.

Sophie was awake. Natalie took her outside and cleaned up the mess in the kitchen. She felt numb. When Sophie barked to be let inside, Natalie opened the door and picked the little dog up in her arms. Sophie licked Natalie's face. She sat down on the floor, hugging the dog to her, and burst into tears.

The phone rang. It was Helen.

"Natalie, are you all right?"

"Yes. I have the will." She couldn't tell her the rest.

"I'll be there in a few minutes. I'm so relieved."

Natalie went upstairs to put on a pair of shoes. She checked her pocket for the keys to Buck's car. It was empty. They must have fallen out when Ron took the pistol away. She couldn't decide whether to wait for Helen or walk back to the dig to get Ron's truck. Would he have left the key in the ignition?

She sat down on the bed, took out the will, and read it. Everything was just as Henry had told her. The old Victorian, the little bungalow, and the ten acres around them went to the family. Harriet wrote that they were worth at least five hundred thousand, and that was enough to leave for two children who were already well off. The pot, which she wrote she and Nathan had purchased on a trip to the Southwest, would go to Ron. Every other artifact went to the native people. The land would be deeded to the Nature Conservancy. A gold locket, in the safety deposit box, went to Natalie, who was also named as executor of the will. Harriet had covered all the angles.

Waldo barked below. Natalie stood and looked out the window. Below, in the driveway, stood Ron. His head was bleeding. He looked dazed. One shoulder hung at an odd angle.

He raised his head toward the window, and she moved aside, knowing he had seen her.

Chapter Twenty-Seven: Axe

Natalie pushed the curtain aside and peered out the window. Ron walked to the woodpile, pulled the ax from the chopping block, and headed for the house. She wanted to run from the house, but there was no way to tell which way he would come in, and a mistake would be fatal. She hesitated. She could lock herself in the bathroom and hope someone would come in time to save her. The odds were slim. She needed a weapon. She hurried to the attic door, opened it quietly, and climbed the stairs.

A faint light shone through a window at one end. In the corner, where Helen had found her teddy bear, the trunk sat open. There was enough standing clutter to create a hiding place. She pulled the string to turn on the light and scanned the room. Surely there was something up here she could use for a weapon. She noticed the archery set, pulled out the bow and examined the string. It was a thirty-pound bow, similar to the one she had used in college archery eons ago. The quiver held six arrows. Three were missing steel tips. Another had only two feathers. She managed to brace the bow against her calf and bend it to attach the string. When she let go, the loop broke.

She heard the front door open and close in the house below. He was inside.

Her hands shook. She tried to make another loop, couldn't manage it. Her shoulder throbbed. She feared she might hyperventilate and pass out. She stopped, closed her eyes, put a hand on her stomach, took a deep breath, let it out slowly. Then another. She took her time to fashion the loop, pulled it tight. She bent the bow and gently attached the string to the notch. It held.

A step creaked on the stairway leading up to the second floor. Ron called to her. She yanked hard on the light bulb string, snapping it as the light went out. That left only the dim light from the window. His eyes would take a minute or two to adjust after he reached the top of the stairs. Grabbing the bow and pair of arrows, she wedged herself between the trunk and a sewing dummy, leaving enough room to draw the bowstring. She tried to recall the last time she had shot a bow and arrow—it had been fifteen years.

The waiting was torture. His footsteps moved from room to room, closet doors creaked, beds scraped across floors. He walked slowly, methodically. He had stopped calling her name.

The attic door creaked open. His footfall on the first step made her heart skip a beat.

Natalie could hear the voice of her Tai Chi instructor, Adrian. "You've lost your center, Nat. Breathe from your center. Pull the energy in through the tan-tien. Here! Let the chi flow through your body." She could feel Adrian poking her below the belly button. She took a deep breath and let it out slowly. Another. Another. Time slowed. She opened her eyes. She heard the crunch of tires in the driveway. Ron stopped moving, probably listening. Time stood still. A feeling of peace descended on her. The dim light filtering in through the window shifted, became yellow, seemed to glow. Another footfall on the stairs, higher up. She gently picked up an arrow, fitted the shaft onto the bow, and drew back.

The profile of his head appeared, then his shoulders. She was afraid to wait for a frontal shot, when he would be in position to charge her if she missed. Better to wound him on the stairs. Her fingers let loose. The arrow flew past his head and clattered onto the floor beyond. He turned to look in her direction, stepped up to the attic floor, the ax in his hand.

"I know you're here now. Why don't you come out so we can finish it," he hissed, barely a whisper.

She felt amazingly calm. She placed the last arrow in the bow, drew it back, waited. He was walking toward her. Twenty feet. Fifteen. She was ready.

A voice called up from below. "Nat, where are you?"

It was Helen. Ron paused. Natalie knew he would kill Helen, too. He listened as Helen's footsteps echoed in the hallway below.

"We're up here, Helen," he called.

"Helen! Stay away. He'll kill you!" Natalie screamed.

She had given herself away. He looked straight at her, eyes filled with rage. He raised the ax and lunged. She took aim, blinked, corrected her angle by an inch, released.

His scream echoed through the room. He stumbled backwards, tugging at the arrow through his neck, then fell to the floor. Natalie dropped the bow.

Helen raced up the stairs. Seeing Ron lying on the floor, she screamed. His body arched, his legs jerked, then he lay still. Natalie stood up. She felt surprisingly calm. Helen looked at her, terrified.

"He killed Harriet, Helen. And he was going to kill me," Natalie said.

She walked over to Ron and felt his pulse. He was unconscious, but still alive. "Stay with him while I call an ambulance." Helen stared at Ron, unable to speak. "Can you handle this, Helen?"

Helen looked up and blinked. "Yes. Go on. Go call."

Chapter Twenty-Eight: Buck

The next morning, Davis lay propped up in a hospital bed looking tired and pale. His wife, Marie, bent over to kiss him. She stood up and smiled at Natalie, who stood in the doorway.

"I have to get back to work," Marie said to Natalie. "Don't let him get out of bed."

"I'm not going to use that stupid little blue pee pot again, Marie. If I have to go, I'm getting up. Nat will help me," Davis said weakly.

"Don't bet on it," Natalie said, walking into the room and sitting down. Marie gave a tiny wave and left. "You need to keep your weight off those ribs for a few days," Natalie said. "How's the pain?"

"Bad. The pills help, but they make me cranky."

"Ron's in the ICU. They don't know if he'll make it. He lost a lot of blood. Helen and I did what we could for him, but it may not have been enough."

"Do you care?"

"Only in the sense that I don't want to be responsible for his death."

"If he dies, the only one responsible is Ron." Buck lifted his head, reached for a glass of water, and took a sip. He groaned as he lay back on the pillow. "It was a stupid thing to do," he said.

"What Ron did?"

"You going after him alone."

"He would have destroyed the will."

"He almost destroyed you."

"I could say it was stupid of you to have thrown yourself in the path of that heifer."

"I saved a child."

"I saved something too. There's no difference."

"Maybe."

"Look, Buck, you were willing to sacrifice yourself without a second thought. The child might have been killed, and you would have carried the image of that death for the rest of your life, wondering why you hesitated."

"That wasn't why I did it. I didn't have time to think."

"Then explain it to me."

"The child, at that moment, was a part of myself. That's all I know. I didn't see the child as separate. What I did was instinctive. That's why heroes don't like to be recognized. Anyone would have done the same thing. You have to be in the situation to understand—something else takes over which can't be resisted."

"I do understand," Natalie said. "For a moment, humanity became more important than Buck Davis. The fate of a place became more important than Nat Hughes. It boils down to the same thing, becoming part of something greater than yourself. We won, Buck. We did it." She gave him her best smile, reached over and patted his hand.

He smiled, tried to lift himself, groaned, fell back. "Somehow I don't feel as good as you do. What about the cave? You said something last night about finding the cave."

"It belongs to the foxes and the past. As far as I'm concerned, it doesn't exist. Harriet wanted Ron to stop the dig because the place was sacred ground. We'll leave it at that. If he recovers, he'll end up in prison."

"And the pot?"

"The story will be that Harriet bought it in New Mexico, years ago. Can I count on you to keep the secret? If it gets out, the entire bluff will be torn apart. Archeologists will pour in from all over the country."

"I have no stake in the thing. No one will know."

"You're a rare bird, Buck. I'm putting you on my life list."

"You'd make a good detective."

"Biologists are detectives."

"What about your job?"

"I'm back on board 'til the regular biologist returns. I'll commute from Clam Beach. The Coast Guard has the kayak. Fish and Wildlife will bring it out for me."

He looked down and fiddled with the pages of a newspaper lying on the bed covers. "Are you going to stay in the area?"

"I think so. I have an aunt who lives an hour's drive away, in the redwoods. I love the bay, but the forest feels like home. I spent my last two years of high school there. When the job runs out, I'll visit her for a couple of weeks, then look around for a job. They need biologists to do spotted owl surveys."

"I see in the paper where a corporate raider just bought a big lumber company and wants to cut all the old growth to pay off the debt. There's an activist named Bigfoot blowing up bridges and running log loaders off cliffs. Don't get tangled up in that mess."

"I don't see what that has to do with me."

"Just saying. Things are getting very nasty up here. It's not like the old days. I have one murder case a month, used to be one a year."

"I think I can take care of myself. And if I can't I know who to call." She patted his hand again.

He frowned at her. "Hand me that little blue pot, please. I need a few moments of privacy."

About the author:

While searching through the effects of my late mother, Sharon Greene, I discovered a completed manuscript, *Medicine Bird*, of which she had frequently spoken but never published. Following an extensive rewrite, the novel will now be published under Sharon's name with all profits donated to her favorite nonprofit organization, Friends of the Van Duzen River.

Sharon lived in Humboldt County, California, which served as the inspiration for the landscapes, characters and events of *Medicine Bird.* She was an avid birdwatcher and painter who devoted her spare time to volunteering with local environmental organizations and teaching Tai Qi. After a long battle with cancer, Sharon passed away in December of 2003.

Jacen Greene
Beaverton, Oregon

www.ingramcontent.com/pod-product-compliance
Lightning Source LLC
LaVergne TN
LVHW090938080826
845145LV00003B/800

* 9 7 8 0 9 8 5 7 6 1 6 1 5 *